Samantha jerked her hand from his grasp

"What do you want? Whenever you pretend to be nice, I know you're softening me up for a favor."

Doug's lips twitched in amusement. "Ever suspicious. The changes are all cosmetic, aren't they? Two years in Europe have added a certain gloss, but inside you're the same old Sam."

"And what was wrong with the old Sam?"

"She was a pest, a pain in the neck, a brat."

"Oh, we're back to the kind of flattery from you that I recognize," she said.

Doug's hands encircled her throat, his thumb tracing her chin line. "You're still a pain in the neck, but with a difference. Your smooth-mouthed insolence used to tempt me to wash your mouth out with soap. Now your mouth tempts me to do something quite, quite different."

Jeanne Allan lived in Nebraska, where she was born and raised, until her marriage to a United States Air Force lieutenant. More than a dozen moves have taken them to Germany and ten different states. Between moves, Jeanne spent time as a volunteer. With her two teenage children, she enjoys nature walks, bird-watching and photography at the family's cabin in the Colorado mountains, and she enjoys all kinds of crafts, including making stained-glass windows. She has always liked to write, but says her husband had to bully her into writing her first romance novel.

Jeanne Allan was named Romance Writer of the Year for 1989 by the Rocky Mountain Fiction Writers.

Books by Jeanne Allan

HARLEQUIN ROMANCE
2845—WHEN LOVE FLIES BY
2875—THE WAITING HEART
2899—THE GAME IS LOVE
2935—TRUST IN LOVE
2989—ONE RECKLESS MOMENT
3073—BLUEBIRDS IN THE SPRING
3121—NO ANGEL
3175—RANCHER'S BRIDE

FROM THE HIGHEST MOUNTAIN
Jeanne Allan

Harlequin Books

TORONTO • NEW YORK • LONDON
AMSTERDAM • PARIS • SYDNEY • HAMBURG
STOCKHOLM • ATHENS • TOKYO • MILAN
MADRID • WARSAW • BUDAPEST • AUCKLAND

Original hardcover edition published in 1991
by Mills & Boon Limited

ISBN 0-373-03217-X

Harlequin Romance first edition September 1992

FROM THE HIGHEST MOUNTAIN

CHAPTER ONE

"I DON'T want to drive Doug home."

"Come on, Sam." David Arden's fond look was tinged with exasperation. "I know Doug's not your favorite person——"

"To say the least," Samantha said.

Her brother eyed her speculatively. "I never have figured out what Doug did for you to dislike him so much."

"I don't dislike him. I just don't share Mom's and your excessively high opinion of him. Why can't Mom drive him?"

"You know Mom is driving Lynda's parents. Mr. and Mrs. Hillard would think it pretty strange if she abandoned them for Doug," David said. His lips tightened. "Never mind. I'll drive Doug's car, and Lynda can drive mine."

"Oh, all right. I'll take him. We can't have the bride and groom driving home from their rehearsal dinner separately." Her mouth turned down at the corners. "Leave it to Doug to be a fly in the ointment."

David gave her a look of mild reproach. "I doubt that Doug deliberately set about giving himself a blinding migraine."

"I wouldn't put it past him." Samantha couldn't remember a time within the last twelve years when Doug wasn't disrupting at least one of her carefully laid plans. Or so it seemed. A two-year separation had not made

5

her heart grow any fonder, and she'd avoided him during the three weeks she'd been home.

Standing shivering beside Doug's locked car after the dinner did little to improve her mood. The night was clear, but towering mountains and looming pines blotted out most of the sky. Where was Doug? If the temperature wasn't below zero, it was close. As was to be expected in the Colorado Rockies in January. She heard the snow crunching beneath his feet before she saw him. "About time," she said as he unlocked the doors.

Doug slid into the passenger side of his four-wheel-drive vehicle. "Thanks for driving me back. I appreciate it. A migraine totally fuzzes up my vision."

Samantha grabbed the keys from his outstretched hand and jammed one in the ignition. "You may as well know that David practically forced me."

"Same old Samantha." His seat belt fastened, Doug leaned his head against the back of the seat, his eyes closed. "Two years in Switzerland doesn't seem to have changed you much. No taller, no sweeter."

"I realize that you prefer women who fawn all over you, women who squeal when they feel your muscles, and women who faint if you condescend to smile in their direction."

"Sure." A slight chuckle rumbled up from his chest. "But, now that you're back home, I won't have to worry about female flattery giving me a swollen head. You're an expert with the deflating jab. It'll be just like old times."

"Not quite. You forget about Lynda."

"No. I haven't forgotten about Lynda." After a minute he said, "I was talking about you and me. The spoiled brat and——"

"Spoiled brat! At least I belonged here. I wasn't some uninvited guest who was always hanging around."

"I didn't realize you still felt that way."

If he were anyone else, Samantha might have thought she detected a tinge of hurt in his voice. But this was Doug. Insensitive, bullheaded, thick-skinned Doug. Savagely she ground the gears of his car.

He winced. "Good Lord, did you forget how to drive while you were in Switzerland?"

"If you don't like the way I drive, you're welcome to go with someone else." She turned angrily toward him. At the sight of his white face, her conscience pricked her. "I'm sorry. Your head's pretty bad, and my driving isn't helping it any, is it?"

One corner of Doug's face turned up in a wry grin. "Don't apologize. It would only disillusion me if I suddenly discovered that you were adhering to the policy that one catches more flies with sugar than vinegar." He paused. "I might even worry since I know that you already consider me one of those pesky insects. A fly in the ointment, I believe you said."

Compassion flew out the window. "You were eavesdropping! David would never in a hundred years have repeated what I said." She turned her attention back to the road just as a large black cat darted across the road. Forgetting the clutch, Samantha slammed on the brakes, sending the car into a dangerous skid at the same moment that the engine coughed and bucked to a halt.

"Of all the stupid..." Doug slumped back in his seat, and the arms that had been bracing him against the dashboard dropped limply into his lap. "I know you don't like me, but don't you think murder is going a little too far?"

"Very funny. Was I supposed to hit the cat?" Her hands still shaking from the sudden fright, she tried to restart the car. In vain.

Doug leaned back against the seat, his eyes closed. "Now you've flooded it." His air of martyrdom was as obvious as a scarlet cloak.

"Thank you, Albert Einstein. I know I flooded it." Pressing the accelerator to the floor, she turned the key. The engine refused to catch.

"You're only making it worse. We'll have to let it sit for a while." Doug straightened up and looked out of the window. "At least we're off the road. We may as well go in the lounge over there and have a drink while we're waiting."

"I'll call David."

"By the time he could get here, the car will start."

Samantha slammed the car door and followed him. "We always have to do things your way, don't we?"

"And you never can admit that my way might be the best way." At the bar, Doug fumbled for the door handle.

She reached around him and opened the door. "That's not true."

"Admit it, Sam. If I told you not to drink poison, you'd do it just to spite me." He slid into the booth across from her.

"Only if everyone would blame you."

Doug ordered for them and then studied her across the table. "I didn't realize until now how tame Breckenridge has seemed without you. Why did you stay away so long?"

She started to snap something sarcastic, but the sight of his drawn face stopped her. Surely they could behave in a civilized manner for one evening? "I came home a couple of times. You just weren't here. And Mom and David came over to Switzerland several times. I missed family and home, but I loved it over there. The Meyers were good to me, and it was a great job-learning experience. The big hotel in Berne and the smaller inn in Lauterbrunnen—I dealt with all kinds of people."

"Now what?"

"I don't know. With my degree in hotel management and my references, I don't expect to have any trouble finding a job. I can always go back to Europe, but I thought I'd stay around and help Mom with the inn for a while. She could use some free time. I've been thinking about moving back to the States for a while now." She shrugged. "Being so far away and all...I mean, I didn't have a clue about David. His engagement was totally unexpected."

"Why unexpected? David is almost thirty." Doug ordered another glass of wine.

"So are you," Samantha said, sipping her coffee. "Where's your bride?"

"She dumped me." Doug lifted his glass of wine in a toast. "To weddings."

Samantha quickly looked down at her cup to hide her surprise. Neither her mother nor her brother had mentioned Doug's being engaged. She wondered who the woman was. Knowing Doug's preferences, someone tall and brainless. Changing the subject, she asked about his headache.

"I took something—new medicine the doctor gave me. It must be working. Those electric snakes that were dancing across your face seem to be gone." He squinted at her over the top of his glass. "Or maybe they're all hiding in those red curls of yours. Things are still a little blurred."

"My hair isn't red—that's the light in here, I'm what's known as a strawberry blonde."

Doug shook his head. "Lynda is blonde. Blonde and beautiful."

"She certainly is beautiful. And she seems so nice. I'm looking forward to getting better acquainted with her. Do you know her well?"

"Oddly enough, no." He took a big swallow. "Considering that I'd planned to marry her."

"Oh." Samantha stared at him in dismay. "I didn't know."

"Why would you? You weren't here. Just me and David. And then Lynda moved to Breckenridge last fall. She reminded me of the ice sculptures for the Ullr Fest: pale, icy." He stared into his glass. "I'd planned to be the fire that melted the goddess of ice." His low voice carried to the next booth, and the people turned to look curiously.

Samantha shifted uneasily on the leather-upholstered seat. "I'm sorry, I——"

"You're sorry. How do you think I feel?" He ground a pretzel into the tabletop. "Her skin looks so smooth and cool. I wanted to touch it. That's all. Just touch it." His eyes filled with pain. "Tomorrow night, David— my best friend, David—will touch that skin. And I'll never know what it would be like to run my lips down her stomach, hold those beautiful snow-white breasts in my hands."

The couple at the next table hung on his words, and Sam inwardly cringed. Doug hadn't had that much to drink. His new medicine must be reacting with the small amount of alcohol he'd consumed. "Don't you think we can go home now?"

Doug shook his head. "I can't. I have to drink a toast to my best friend." Enunciating carefully, he gave her an owlish look. "He's getting married tomorrow, you know."

"I know." Great. The bartender was looking in their direction. Now what was she supposed to do?

"How do you know?" Doug asked.

"David is my brother."

"Brother. Here's to brothers."

Samantha sighed. David, I'll get you for this, she promised silently. Why hadn't her brother told her that Doug was in love with Lynda? She gave a quick negative shake of her head to the waitress who hesitated as she passed their table. A whiff of perfume smelling like fly spray assaulted Samantha's nose. The irritating whir of a blender sounded from behind the bar as she grappled with the problem of getting Doug home.

"You didn't drink to your brother," he accused her. "Don't you love him?"

"Of course I love him." She lifted her cup. "To brothers. To friends. And to weddings. One of which we both have to attend tomorrow. I don't know about you, but I need my beauty sleep. Let's go."

Doug was still contemplating his drink. "Go ahead."

"I can't. I promised my brother I'd drive you home." For which he shall pay, she added to herself.

Doug slapped some money on the table and stumbled to his feet. "Sisters. Damned worthless appendages."

She bundled him into the passenger side of his car and breathed a silent prayer of thanksgiving as the engine started up immediately. Cautiously she turned on to

Breckenridge's main street. The small town sparkled with light. Hundreds of tiny bulbs outlined shop windows and roofs and were strung through small trees along the pavement, while old-fashioned-looking street lamps cast a rosy glow over piles of snow. The shops were closed for the night but brightly lit windows drew passersby who peered at the enticing goods displayed within.

"Sammie, don't ever fall hopelessly in love," Doug muttered at her side. "It hurts too bad."

"Okay." A maudlin drunk she ought to be able to handle, she thought even as she wondered at his revelations. Doug wasn't the confiding type; nor did he take kindly to losing. Even to David. "Does David know how you feel?"

"David's my friend. I introduced them. Showing off my beautiful blonde. I could tell immediately that he liked Lynda, and I was pleased." He gave a bitter laugh. "I was a fool."

"They seem so right for each other. They're good together."

That bitter laugh again. "Good together. In bed. Out of bed. In bed. Out of bed."

He repeated the words in a drunken singsong voice until Samantha wanted to scream at him to shut up. Her mind raced furiously. David hated to cause pain, yet his happiness appeared totally unmarred by any misgivings. He couldn't possibly be aware of Doug's unrequited passion. It appeared that at least Doug had had the decency to conceal his feelings from David.

She glanced over at her passenger. Doug's head rested against the seat back with his mouth gaping open. In spite of the freezing January night, both his topcoat and suit jacket hung open. He'd unbuttoned the collar of his shirt, and a tie dangled from the breast pocket.

Samantha considered him as she drove. This must be the first time that Douglas Patton Clayborne Jr. had found himself in a situation that he couldn't handle. She remembered the first time David had brought Doug home. Doug had looked down on David's sister with an air of superiority that only an eighteen-year-old college freshman could achieve, at the same time treating Mrs. Arden with a teasing courtesy that quickly had her eating out of his hand. David couldn't praise his new friend and roommate enough. The small-town boy worshiping the sophisticate. Doug's father was in the Air Force, and Doug had lived and traveled all over the world.

From the heights of her twelve-year-old wisdom, Samantha had doubted that they'd ever see Doug again once he met more people at school, but she'd been wrong. Vacation after vacation, holiday after holiday, Doug had trailed home after David. It was too expensive to join his parents in England, or by the time he'd told them his vacation dates they were already booked on a Greek cruise. There had always been some excuse. Made up, Samantha was convinced, because Doug liked the way Mrs. Arden spoiled the boys when they came home. Nobody had considered how Samantha felt. The brother who had used to take her everywhere now went with Doug. Doug, who had convinced her brother that allowing a little sister to tag along with them was a drag as well as a hindrance to any kind of social life. Social life meaning girls.

She'd heard Doug's arguments during his first visit to their home. They were the opening salvo of a war that the two of them had waged on each other for years, Doug more subtly than Samantha. He had always brought her a present, being sure that he gave it to her in front of her mother, forcing her to thank him civilly when they both knew she hated the gift. Paper dolls when she was too old for them, girlish stationery when she hated to write letters, hair bows she never wore and stockings with lace on them. What tomboy needed lacy stockings? The gift she'd hated the most, and for which she'd never forgiven him, had been a book. The title was forgotten but not the premise: how to be popular even if you weren't beautiful. Doug had given her the book right after Tony Asher had asked Susie Smythe to the Junior Prom. Susie Smythe, who had been afraid of worms and couldn't climb a tree.

Samantha drove around to the back of the three Victorian homes which made up the Hummingbird Inn and pulled into Doug's parking place. Opening the passenger door, she shook him awake. "Come on, Sleeping Beauty."

Doug and David shared the top floor of the third and latest-acquired house. Finding the key in Doug's pocket, Samantha let them in the back door. The bottom floor was still vacant and the middle floor was Doug's studio, so there was no one to see as Doug stumbled slowly up the staircase. David wasn't home yet, so Samantha was forced to help Doug into his bedroom where she managed to remove his topcoat before he slumped onto the bed. Now what? She tossed her coat on a nearby chair. Impossible to simply abandon him. Suppose... The sudden disquieting thought sent her scrambling on her knees across his bed. She ripped open his shirt and placed her hand on his chest. His heart beat steadily. His skin was smooth as silk and burned her palm.

Doug grabbed her hand, tugging it toward his mouth, where his lips nuzzled her wrist. "You smell good. Like a summer meadow with soft breezes blowing through the wildflowers."

Samantha froze in astonishment at Doug's unexpected action and words. Before she could react, he was nibbling a path up her forearm. Who would have guessed that teeth could be so erotic? She shook her head to rid herself of such thoughts. Was she crazy? Allowing Doug Clayborne to slobber all over her. There was no time to pursue that thought as Doug pulled her down to his level. "What do you think you're doing?" she said, pushing against his chest.

He laughed softly, ignoring her puny efforts to escape as he wove his fingers through her hair. "Your lips don't look so icy." He rolled over on top of her, pressing her into the mattress.

"Douglas Clayborne, you get off me this instant or——"

His mouth swallowed the rest of her threat. It seemed her very breath was being swallowed by his kiss. Not that Doug was forcible or demanding. On the contrary—his lips were gentle. And persuasive. Outside car doors slammed and voices carried on the night air. In the bedroom there were the sounds of breathing, the beating of hearts, the creaking of bed springs. Doug slid his lips over hers. Samantha could taste the wine he'd drunk earlier. The fists beating against his chest slowed, and suddenly her hands were gripping his shoulders, feeling the tense play of muscles beneath her touch.

"Not so icy, after all." His lips moved over hers. "Lynda. Lovely, lovely Lynda."

Samantha turned to stone. In his wine-and-medicine-induced stupor, Doug didn't even know whom he was kissing. "Get off me," she gritted through clenched teeth. Anger gave her strength, and she shoved him to one side.

He chuckled, a heartless sound. "Don't play games. You enjoyed that as much as I did." He reached for her. "Lynda."

"I'm not Lynda." Sitting up, she rearranged her clothing.

Doug squinted at her. "Where's Lynda? What have you done with Lynda?" His voice rose with the last question.

In the other room, a door slammed. David was home. He could take care of Doug. Then Doug muttered Lynda's name again, and Samantha's first rush of relief died away. If David heard and interpreted what Doug was saying... She put her finger over Doug's lips. "It's Samantha. I'm here with you."

Eyes shut, Doug stubbornly shook his head back and forth. "Not Sam. Lynda. Want Lynda." His voice grew louder.

Samantha could hear David's footsteps drawing nearer, and her hand pressed over Doug's mouth. David must not learn about this—not now, not the night before his wedding. David was so happy. Doug shook off her hand. Before he could open his mouth, Samantha flopped over on top of him. If she couldn't shut him up one way, she'd have to do it another.

At least this way he cooperated—with more enthusiasm than she would have liked. Perhaps he could be excused for thinking the enthusiasm was mutual since every time he tried to say something Samantha pressed her lips against his. Doug's arms wrapped around her waist, imprisoning her on top of his firm body. She dared not fight. Not with her brother still moving about in the other room. Go to bed, David! Mentally castigating her brother, it was a moment before she realized that Doug had taken advantage of her inattention to trade positions with her so that she was on her back. His hands were busy with the buttons of her silk dress. "What do you think you're doing?" she spat.

"Stay with me. Just for tonight, Lynda."

The name seemed to peal loudly through the room. Samantha yanked Doug's mouth back down to hers. He took the kiss as a sign of permission to continue his quest. The first hesitant touch of his fingers against her breast made her gasp. Surely Doug couldn't make her feel like this? Her body was warm and melting, her breast swelling to fill his palm. Doug laid his head on her shoulder as he toyed with a hardening nipple. She could feel his warm breath caressing her skin even as she forgot how to breathe.

"So beautiful. So smooth. Like silk. You smell good." Doug's voice died away. His hand clenched convulsively about her breast and then lay heavily on her chest, cupping the full mound. A loud snore reverberated through the bedroom.

Samantha fought to control the quick beating of her heart. How could Doug fall asleep now? Reality flooded back, bringing relief. Who knew what he would have thought of next? His arm was warm and heavy against her flesh, but until she was certain he wouldn't awaken she dared not move it. Not with David roaming about in the other room.

David finally went to bed, and the apartment was silent. Now was her chance to escape. Samantha slid carefully from beneath Doug's arm and eased off the bed. Her hand was on the doorknob before an unwelcome thought stopped her. Prescribed medication and alcohol could be a deadly combination. Sneaking away and leaving Doug was unconscionable. If he didn't wake in the morning... She briefly considered waking David and explaining. No. David was getting married tomorrow. Not only did he need his rest, but there was always the possibility that Doug would partially rouse and disclose his feelings about Lynda. That would be disastrous. Her mother would sit with Doug, but she'd wonder why Samantha couldn't handle the situation herself. Especially as Mrs. Arden was probably fast asleep while Samantha was right here. She grimaced at the slumbering figure on the bed. As usual, Doug was being a perfect pain in the neck.

The room contained a bed and one wooden chair. Samantha refused to sit up all night. As for her clothes, her silk dress had been purchased with too many Swiss francs in Berne to consider sleeping in it. Slipping out of it, she hung it in Doug's wardrobe. Impossible to sleep in anything so constricting as tights, and they were discarded next. Clad in her slip, she padded on bare feet to the bed. Slowly she eased Doug's shoes from his feet and then unfolded the blanket from the foot of the bed and spread it over him. Moving quietly around the bed, she slid under the covers.

Dawn was picking out the shapes of the furniture when Samantha awakened after a restless night. Sleeping with Doug snoring in her ear had been hopeless. More disturbing had been the fact that her every movement seemed to bring her into contact with Doug's hard body. The bed covers separated them, but that didn't spare Samantha from recalling Doug's embrace each time they touched.

He was sleeping quietly and would be perfectly all right if she left him now. He need never know that she'd spent the night beside him. His chagrin at her discovering his weakness would be equaled only by his ridicule when he realized she'd been worried about him. If there was any justice in this world, he'd awake with a king-size hangover.

She slid from the bed. The room was freezing, the lining of her coat icy against bare skin. Her clothes were quickly bundled up. She tiptoed from the room and slowly shut the door, scarcely daring to breathe as she cautiously turned the doorknob until it caught with a barely perceptible click. Letting her breath out with a sigh, Samantha turned to face the room.

"Good morning."

Samantha instinctively pressed a finger against her lips for silence, her stomach taking an apprehensive dip. The look on her brother's face left no doubt that she was not leaving the apartment without giving him a satisfactory explanation. "Good morning. Is there more coffee?" she asked, putting off the inevitable.

David pointed to the chair across the table from him and handed her a mug. "Well?"

"It's not what you think?"

"What do I think?"

"You think that Doug and I...we didn't and we weren't," she ended with a rush.

David's sharp gaze went from her face to the bundle of clothing she clutched on her lap. "Don't tell me Mother had to rent out your room last night."

"You needn't be sarcastic. There's a perfectly good explanation for—for this."

"'This' being why you're coming from Doug's bedroom at six-thirty in the morning wearing only your underwear and a coat."

"Yes." She took a sip of coffee, frantically editing the story in her mind.

"Well?" David's face was stony beneath his tousled blond curls.

Samantha set her mug on the table. "I flooded the engine on the way home so we went in for a drink to let it set for a few minutes." She explained about the effect of Doug's new medication and his two glasses of wine. "I couldn't just leave him alone after he passed out."

"Doug's car was here when I got home. You must have been in his room when I came in. Why didn't you holler at me?"

"I must have fallen asleep," she lied. This was the sticky part. "Besides, today's your wedding day. You needed your sleep." She tried a teasing grin. "I can catch up on my sleep tonight. I won't be on my honeymoon."

Color flagged David's cheeks, but he ignored her implication. "Now let's hear the part you're leaving out."

"I don't know what you mean."

"You've never been a very good liar." David studied her over his mug. Suddenly a huge grin split his face. "Of course. You and Doug." He leaned back and slapped the table. "I've suspected for years that you had a crush on him. Finally wore him down, did you?"

"I don't know what you mean," Samantha repeated stiffly.

"And you have me to thank. Pretending you didn't want to drive Doug home." David crowed with laughter. "When did it finally happen? When you were stranded and had to actually talk to each other?"

"Don't be silly. Doug and I . . . the whole idea is preposterous." The memories of Doug's kisses and the warm feel of his hand on her breast flooded over her. She refused to look at her brother, but she knew that the sudden flush on her face betrayed her.

"You can't fool your old brother." David's voice was colored with equal parts of amusement and triumph.

"He really did pass out from the medicine and the wine," Samantha insisted.

"I'm sure he did. Just as I'm sure the old Sam would have promptly dumped him on his bed, notified her older brother, and waltzed blithely off to bed, praying that Doug would awaken with one tremendous hangover. The new Sam, one who's finally admitted Doug's sterling qualities, tucked him lovingly into bed and maintained a bedside vigil throughout the night."

"That's not true——"

David wasn't listening to her. "Wait until I tell Lynda."

"No, don't——"

"For a minute there, I thought I might have to bust my old friend in the chops for compromising my little sister, but this is different."

Samantha's hands froze around her coffee mug. What had she got herself into? If she convinced David that she and Doug didn't care for each other, he'd probe deeper and deeper into her actions. And he was right. She'd never been very good at lying to him. Easier to go along with him now—later she could explain. After the honeymoon. When it no longer mattered because David and Lynda would be safely married. She gave her brother a weak smile. "We wanted to keep it a secret."

"Why?"

She hunched one shoulder defensively. "Today belongs to Lynda. It wouldn't be fair if we stole some of her thunder by announcing..." The words caught in her throat.

"You're engaged?" David's grin grew even wider.

"No! That is, not really. Please, David. Keep our secret." She twisted the mug in her hands. "It's not fair to either Lynda or me to make us share the spotlight. Let her have her hour and then...later..."

David shook his head in resigned amusement. "You never have liked sharing the center of attention."

"It's settled, then? You won't tell?"

"Scout's honor." He followed the pledge with the ritual. "Your secret is safe with me."

"What secret?"

Samantha turned in horror. Doug was leaning against the doorjamb to his bedroom. Even from this distance she could see his drooping eyelids.

Before she could intercept him, David leapt to his feet and was across the room shaking Doug's hand enthusiastically. "You sly dog, you. Congratulations."

Doug winced and covered his eyes with his other hand. "What the hell are you talking about?" Recovering his hand from David, he stumbled across the room and poured himself some coffee and drank it as if he'd been dry for a week. Pouring a second cup, he turned and his gaze landed on Samantha. His brows lifted at the state of her undress. "Congratulations for what?"

"What Sam just told me." David chortled with delight. Encountering Samantha's fierce look, he backed toward his bedroom, his hands raised in surrender. "Okay. I won't say another word. Except that I thoroughly approve."

Doug dropped heavily into a chair across from Samantha. "I'm not a well man, and I have a feeling I'm going to feel even worse when I find out what your brother is talking about."

Revenge is sweet, Samantha thought. She gave Doug a demure smile. "I suppose that all brothers get excited when they learn that their sister's just got engaged."

"Congratulations. Who's the poor, unlucky devil?"

Samantha toasted him with her coffee mug.

Doug choked on his coffee. "Wait a minute. You're not saying that you and I... Impossible!"

She fluttered her eyelashes at him and heaved a rapturous sigh. "You were so romantic. I was simply swept off my feet."

"What the hell are you talking about?" He slammed his mug on the table. "What's going on?"

Samantha was thankful that she could hear David's shower. The noise of running water would drown out Doug's yelling. She shot an icy glare across the table. "Let me put it this way: any lipstick on your collar is not Lynda's."

"I know..." A startled look replaced the irritation on his face. "What happened last night?"

"To begin with, I'm not the one who made a fool of myself."

"I don't remember much about what happened——"

"I'm not surprised."

"But I'm sure," he continued doggedly, "you'll be more than happy to tell me, sparing none of the gruesome details."

Samantha quickly sketched in the events of the previous evening, neglecting to mention everything that had happened once she'd got Doug to his bedroom. The look on Doug's face grew more and more ominous as her recitation faltered to an end. "And when David caught me sneaking from your room this morning, he jumped to a conclusion."

"Which you didn't bother to straighten out."

"I tried, but..."

"But the opportunity to see me twisting in the wind was too tempting to pass up."

"I wasn't thinking of you at all. I——"

"I can believe that," Doug said. "Well, now that you've had your fun, you can tell David the truth."

"No. Not until he and Lynda get back from their honeymoon."

"If you think that I'm going to pretend to be in love with you just because your brother——"

"Caught me sneaking out of your room because I spent the night in there. Worrying about you!"

"I didn't ask you to stay."

"Yes, you did," Samantha said. She faced him boldly across the table. "You begged me."

"You're lying."

"Am I? You remember it so well?"

"You know damned good and well I don't remember much of anything after we went into the lounge." He kicked back his chair and stood up. "I'm going to tell David the truth."

"Fine." Samantha stood up, too. "Tell David the truth." She was trembling with anger. "Tell him how much in love with his bride you are. Tell him how you assaulted his sister because you thought you were making love to his fiancée. If you're lucky, he'll call off the wedding. That's what you want, isn't it? The wedding canceled. Go ahead. Tell him. What are you waiting for?"

CHAPTER TWO

DOUG dropped heavily down onto the chair, horror dulling his eyes as he stared at Samantha. "I assaulted you last night?" He cradled his head in his hands and moaned softly. "Oh, no. I can't believe it." He looked up, pain written all over his face. "You're right. Of course, we'll get married. It's the least I can do." He shook his head. "I'm sorry. I realize that doesn't help much..."

Samantha heaved a sigh of exasperation as she sat back down. Leave it to Doug to pounce on the one thing she shouldn't have said. "This is ridiculous. You don't have to marry me. It wasn't that kind of assault."

"What other kind is there?" he asked, staring into his mug.

"You just kissed me a couple of times." She drew little lines on the table with her finger. "It wasn't what you did, it was why you did it."

That brought his head up. "Would you care to explain?" he asked in a tight voice.

"Not really, but I guess I better. You thought I was Lynda."

His eyes narrowed. "Lynda?"

"You went on and on and on about her last night." Samantha couldn't meet his gaze. "About how beautiful she is and—and..." she took a deep breath "...how you wanted to be her lover..."

26

"I see." Doug stood up abruptly and walked over to the sliding doors off the veranda. The curtains were open, and across the way snow-covered peaks were kissed by the sun's first rays of morning. The ski runs were slashes of gray down the timbered mountains. This early the mountainside still belonged to the birds and the animals. Later would come the shrill cries and slashing skis. While the Ardens were in church.

"I suppose you think it's a good joke." Doug didn't turn around. The suit he'd slept in was rumpled, and he was in his stockinged feet, but the sartorial shortcomings failed to hide a hard, lean physique.

Samantha shook her head at his back. "I wasn't even tempted to laugh."

"Why not?" He turned around. "I wouldn't think you'd miss an opportunity like this to make a fool of me."

"You don't need me for that," she retorted. "Anyway, it's not exactly like short-sheeting your bed or buttering your doorknob."

Doug have a short laugh. "Or putting worms in my shoes."

"I'd forgotten about that." A little giggle slipped out. "And I didn't think I'd ever forget the look on your face."

Doug ran fingers through his already rumpled dark brown hair. "You always were a brat." It wasn't said with affection. "But I never thought you were cruel."

"Thank you for the kind words. Does that mean you'll absolve me of malice? Besides," she added in a begrudging voice, "I owe you for hiding your feelings from David. I-it was kind of you, and I won't forget it."

"That stuck in your throat, didn't it? What makes you think I was being kind to David? Maybe I just didn't want him pitying me." He walked across the room and grabbed her chin, forcing her to look up at him. "I don't want your pity either, so get that look out of your eyes."

She jerked away. "I wouldn't waste my time feeling sorry for you. Besides, Lynda isn't your type."

"Now I suppose I'm going to have to listen to advice for the lovelorn." He sprawled in a chair next to her and contemplated his stockinged feet. "Well, go ahead. What do you suggest to the bachelor who's head over heels n love with his best friend's prospective wife?"

"Find somebody else. Somebody single."

"How original. Why didn't I think of that?"

"You did," Samantha mocked. "We're engaged, remember?" Doug responded with a string of swear words that made her laugh. When he stood up and walked toward David's bedroom, her laughter stopped abruptly. She dashed across the room and barred his way. "What are you doing?"

"I'm going to tell David the truth."

"You can't. I already tried. It's too complicated. He's bound to figure out there's more than we're telling, and then all this about Lynda will come out, and you know you don't want him to know. David would be devastated to discover how you feel. You'll ruin the whole wedding, even if he doesn't feel compelled to postpone it or even call it off. If you're really his friend, you'll keep your mouth shut and go along with this. What's the harm? I made David promise not to tell anyone. We only have to pretend for him today and then he'll be gone. When he gets back from Hawaii, we'll tell him we changed our minds."

Doug grabbed her arms to remove her from his path.

"I thought I heard you two whispering out here. What's going on?" David spoke from behind Samantha. She hadn't heard his door open.

Giving Doug a beseeching look, she said, "Doug is being stubborn about keeping our secret. He wants to tell the world now instead of waiting for tomorrow, but I don't think it's fair to Lynda."

David stepped around her, slapping Doug on the back as he passed. "I'm with you. Shout it from the highest mountain. That's how I felt when Lynda said yes."

Samantha felt Doug stiffen, and his fingers tightened around her arms. She quickly said, "Fine. Do what you want." She sniffed artistically. "It doesn't sound much like love if a fiancé won't even do one little thing that his fiancée wants. In fact, if Doug is going to be so stubborn..." she resisted looking at him "...I'm going to call off our engagement right now."

Doug pulled her up against his hard body. "Oh, no," he said softly. "You aren't going to get off that easy."

Bending his head, he covered her mouth with his. She couldn't fight him. Not with David standing there. A fact that Doug took full advantage of, his tongue immediately thrusting between her lips in a display of sheer masculine dominance. Samantha wanted to slap him. Instead she was forced to play his game. Her body softened and she leaned against him, her hands curving around his neck. Doug slid his hands up her arms and cupped her face, his fingers weaving through her curls while his tongue and lips worked their magic. He was stirring up feelings that she didn't want stirred up. She ought to break away, but instead curled her tongue around his, setting off a chain reaction of sensations that flashed through her body until they formed a molten pool of desire deep within her. David was forgotten. Why they were kissing was forgotten. All she knew was a need so strong, so compelling... Doug wrenched his lips from hers. She stared at him in confusion. His face told her nothing.

Behind them, David cleared his throat. "Well, I guess that settles that," he said, satisfaction oozing from his voice. "Now, the question is, do I announce it or not?"

"No." Samantha couldn't help the pleading look in her eyes.

Doug's thumbs caressed her arms. "We'll let Sam have her way. This time." David walked into the kitchen, and Doug lowered his voice, his next words intended for her alone. "What a pity I wasn't conscious last night. I didn't realize what I was missing."

Samantha struggled to break free of his grasp. "Yes, what a pity, because now you'll only have one kiss from me to remember the rest of your life."

"I wouldn't count on that." An unpleasant smile curled one side of his mouth. "By the way, who put the brakes on?"

Samantha gave him a puzzled frown. "You mean when your car died?"

"No. In my bed last night. You said we were kissing. It was obvious just now that you'd have been willing to kiss all day."

"I would not——"

"So how do I know that, last night...?" Her coat hung open, and Doug's gaze took in her slip before returning to her face. "Are you sure we didn't...?"

"Yes," she said loudly. The quizzical lift of his brow doubted her denial, and without thinking she blurted out, "You fell asleep."

His howl of laughter followed her out the door.

The minister smiled. "You may kiss the bride."

Heat flushed Samantha's face as she remembered Doug's kiss this morning. Involuntarily she glanced across the aisle at the best man. Her heart sank at the look of yearning on Doug's face, but anger quickly shoved aside sympathy. Doug must not be allowed to come between David and Lynda. As he had tried to come between David and Samantha. Deliberately Samantha dropped her bouquet. Ignoring the muffled titters from behind her, she stooped down to pick up her flowers, watching Doug from the corners of her eyes. As she'd hoped, her performance had distracted his attention from the bridal couple.

Straightening up, she fluttered her eyelashes shamelessly at him, adding a demure smile out of pure devilment. Doug's eyes promised retribution. As if she was afraid of him! Arrogant male. His conceit irritated her as much as her own stupidity. How could she have allowed him to think that only his falling asleep last night had curtailed their passion? He'd never let her forget it. Which spelled out their entire relationship—always striving to best the other. Always striving to be first with David.

Lynda reached for her bridal bouquet, bestowing a dazzling smile on Samantha. Her new sister-in-law was a breathtaking bride with ash-blond hair that turned in just above her chinline, accentuating her high cheekbones. Lynda was tall, her soft gray eyes, sparkling with happiness, on the same level as the blue eyes of her new husband.

Doug offered Samantha his arm, and they followed the bridal couple down the aisle. Happiness and love for her brother filled Samantha's heart. Six years apart in age, they were close in companionship and appearance. The same pointed chin, the same well-shaped nose, the same wide mouth. David's curly hair was light without Samantha's reddish cast. Their mother liked to say that David was like old, comfortable, snuggly bedroom slippers.

Her mother also liked to say that the Ardens were built low to the ground. Samantha's five feet four felt dwarfed by Doug's six feet. She could feel the tense muscles of his arm through his formal wool suit and knew he was thinking of the woman he followed down the aisle. The woman he had no right to love. She pinched his arm. Hard. "I hope," she said in a sugary voice, "that you don't still have that sickening look on your face."

Doug pinned her hand between his arm and body. "And I hope..." his voice was just as falsely amiable "...that some day someone teaches you to behave yourself."

Samantha spoke out of the corner of her mouth as she smiled at an old friend. "At least I'm not wishing lightning would come down and strike David dead."

Doug missed a step before he growled, "No. You're wishing it would strike me dead." Before she could deny it, he added, "Maybe that's because it was my dead body that turned you on."

She tried to ease his tight grip. "Let's say I prefer it. So much easier to ignore."

"Does that mean you find my live body irresistible?" He squeezed her hand tighter.

Samantha nodded at an acquaintance. "The word is loathsome." They posed obediently for the photographer at the end of the aisle.

Doug's Cheshire cat grin matched hers. "If you think I'm loathsome, how do you kiss a man you like?"

"With or without my brother watching?" she asked, barely moving her lips.

"That's right. We mustn't let David discover the truth. You can count on me." His voice rang with sincerity.

Samantha gave him a suspicious look. The innocent look on his face might have fooled her, but the angry gleam in his eyes warned her. Doug despised her for learning his secret. Too late it dawned on her that he intended to make her pay.

Their battle raged all afternoon. A silent battle, with only the two combatants aware that it was taking place. Doug started it in the receiving line at the reception. A hand draped casually around her waist slipped down to cup her hip with intimate familiarity. Samantha glared at him.

He gave her an innocent smile. "David's watching," he said in an undertone.

Samantha hastily turned her glare into a smile. "Keep your hands to yourself."

Doug grinned down at her. "David knows me too well to believe that."

"You mean he knows you're a pervert?"

His elbow dug in her side. "Mrs. Garvy—I don't believe you've met David's sister, Samantha Arden. Sam,

Mrs. Garvy moved here from Texas last year and took over the gift shop from Ted Bellows."

The older woman unleashed a charming smile on Samantha. "Your mother has told me all about your working in Switzerland. You're so brave to go halfway across the world all by yourself." She arched her brows at Doug. "We'll have to make sure that she stays home now that we've got her here."

"I'm not sure Sam can take Breckenridge's competition," Doug said with a wink in Mrs. Garvy's direction.

"Silly boy," she said. "If I were ten years younger, I might take you up on that." She moved on.

"Twenty years," Samantha muttered, irked by the childish byplay. No wonder Lynda preferred David to Doug. "I can't believe the way you pandered to that old woman's vanity. You wouldn't catch David sinking that low."

Before Doug could answer her, the reception line broke up, and Lynda and David stopped beside them. "Better watch out, Douglas, my friend. Mrs. Garvy is gearing up to matchmake and..." David grinned in Samantha's direction "...Doug is dead in her sights."

"Your warning comes too late," Doug said. "She took one look at Sam, and one could almost see the wedding bells playing in her mind."

"I've always said Mrs. Garvy has second sight," David laughed.

Lynda giggled. "Isn't her hat outrageously wonderful? David told her if he'd seen her in it earlier he'd have married her instead of me."

Samantha steadfastly refused to look at Doug. He snaked one arm around her and pulled her back against his chest. His hand spread out over her stomach, the heat of his palm burning her through her dress. It took all of her willpower to keep from stamping her heel down on Doug's instep. He hadn't liked her comparing him unfavorably with David, and now he was taking advantage of David's presence to get even. If he could play dirty, so could she. "I haven't kissed the groom yet." Stepping from Doug's embrace, she hugged David enthusiastically and gave him a huge kiss. She turned to smile at Doug. "Aren't you going to kiss the bride?"

Giving her only one deadly glance, Doug rested his hands on Lynda's shoulders and smiled down at her before bestowing a cool kiss on her cheek. "It seems silly to offer you the best when you already have the best in David, but I do."

Lynda gave him a faint smile. "Thank you." She was pale.

Samantha's heart plunged to her toes. Lynda knew Doug was in love with her. Her gaze flew to David—he was laughing at some quip of Doug's. He didn't know. Samantha turned back to Lynda. Her new sister-in-law was staring at her with a faintly accusing air. Samantha felt hot color tinting her face. Lynda suspected that the kiss had been deliberately engineered. And she thought that Samantha had done it to disconcert her. Samantha swallowed hard and rushed into speech. "I'm sorry that your sister couldn't make it to the wedding."

"Jill will never forgive herself for catching chicken pox at the ripe old age of twenty-three. It was kind of you to step in at the last minute to take her place." Lynda's voice was cool.

"It was just lucky that the dress fitted and only had to be shortened," Samantha said. "Not that it would have mattered. You made such a beautiful bride that I could have been wearing a gunny sack and no one would have noticed. Lynda..." Samantha took the other woman's hands in hers "...I want to tell you how happy I am that David found you, and I hope that we can be friends."

Samantha's obvious sincerity dispelled the chill. Lynda hugged her. "I'm sure we will be. David's sister would have to be special. To tell you the truth, I was nervous about meeting you. The way David and Doug talk about you...it's rather intimidating. Is there anything you can't do?"

"Sing." Doug and David spoke in unison.

Lynda looked from one to the other. "A family joke?"

"Not if you have to stand beside her in church," Doug said.

"Or listen to her in the shower," David added.

"You'd better watch out, or I'll sing for your guests," Samantha threatened.

David shivered ostentatiously. "No, no. Not that. Doug, as best man, it's your duty to protect the groom from all evils. Go stuff Sam's mouth with food." A teasing grin lit up his face. "I'm sure you can figure out some way to keep her quiet."

Doug's grin matched David's. "I'll think of something."

An implacable arm at her waist marched Samantha around the corner into an empty hallway. "Where...what are you doing?"

"What your brother expects me to do. Kissing you." Doug's grip held her prisoner.

"That's what you think." She tried to remove the arm at her waist. "You're just trying to get even with me for making you kiss Lynda."

"What's the matter?" he taunted. "Isn't the game as much fun when you're the target? Personally, I'm having

a hell of a good time.'' There was anger in the eyes that
glittered down at her.

She'd gone too far. Samantha opened her mouth to
apologize, but it was too late. Doug yanked her up
against his chest, at the same time pinning her arms
behind her waist. She hastily averted her head, denying
him her mouth. Doug laughed and pushed her back
against the wall so that he only needed one hand to snare
both of hers. His other hand encircled her throat, his
palm resting on the pulse at the base of her neck. ''Such
a rapid pulse,'' Doug said. ''Frightened at what you
stirred up?''

''You don't scare me.''

''No? If it's not fright, then it must be something else.''
His hand slid across the bare skin above her neckline
before edging slowly down to brush against the tip of
one breast.

Samantha tried to block out the sensations that he
was creating even as she felt her breast swell. ''Stop it.''

Doug's hand closed around her breast. ''Why? We're
practically engaged.'' His hips anchored her against the
wall. ''A man likes to know that he can arouse the
woman who's going to share his marriage bed.''

The crude remark brought her head sharply up. ''I'm
not going——'' She should have remembered how
devious he was. His mouth was firm against hers. Voices
and party noises came from the room behind them. The
mingled fragrances of fresh carnations and full-blown
roses were overlaid with the scent of musk. Doug tasted
of mint. The kiss was deep, his lips and tongue triumphant conquerors. At some point he must have released her hands because they were entwined in his hair.
The stiffening flowed from her bones until she was solely
supported by the wall and Doug's body.

He lifted his head. "Had enough?"

Samantha tried to deny the effect his kiss had on her. "What would you do if I said no?"

Doug chuckled. "I never could get you to cry 'Uncle,' could I?"

His amusement swept away the cobwebs that ensnared her reason, and she dropped her lashes to hide a storm of conflicting emotions: the desire which Doug had aroused; anger that he, of all men, could do so; relief that he had not taken her answer seriously; and regret that a passion so easily aroused was fraudulent, based on nothing more than chemistry. And, finally, guilt, and the unhappy realization that she'd brought the whole episode on herself by exploiting her knowledge of Doug's painful secret. "I'm sorry. What I did, forcing you to kiss Lynda, was cruel and unforgivable. I don't blame you for being angry."

"Damn you, don't apologize."

Her startled gaze flew upward. "Why not?"

"Because I hate that little trick where your bottom lip wobbles. The first time I came home with David twelve years ago, you did it, and you've been doing it ever since. You are spoiled rotten and will seemingly go to any length to get your own way or exact your revenge, but just when I decide that you are totally incorrigible something within you seems to bring you to a screeching awareness of your own inequities, and you apologize. And that pathetic little wobble always makes me feel like some kind of monster."

"Then it works, doesn't it?"

He uttered a harsh laugh. "That's what I thought at first. That it was a trick designed to manipulate your victim, but then I realized you were sincerely repentant.

I should have known anyone related to your mother and brother couldn't be all bad.''

"I'm sure Mother and David would be flattered by your high opinion of them."

A hand under her chin lifted her face for his perusal. "That's much better. An insolent Sam I can handle." He gave an exaggerated shiver. "A repentant one turns my bones to jelly."

"You realize you've given me a weapon," Samantha said.

"Nope." Doug grinned. "I haven't. I've studied that little apologetic wobble for the better part of twelve years, and there's one thing I'm pretty sure about. It's not yours to command." He pulled a handkerchief from his pocket. "Do I have any lipstick on me?" When she shook her head, he said, "Neither do you. Go fix your face." She opened her mouth to dispute his right to boss her around, and his grin took on an impudent cast. "Unless you want me to kiss you again."

When Samantha returned to the reception, David and Lynda were preparing to cut the wedding cake. Doug was standing against a far wall watching the hilarious proceedings, a smile on his face. A casual acquaintance would have no trouble believing that Doug was thoroughly enjoying the scene. Samantha knew better. And, if she knew better, then so would David. She made her way through the crowd to Doug's side and slipped her arm through his. "Poor little dog lose his bone?"

His smile slipped a centimetre. "When it comes to miracles, you make a believer out of a man."

"That much of an improvement?" She lifted her face for his inspection. "It's amazing what a little makeup will do."

"I was referring to the fact that you've reached the ripe old age of twenty-four without being murdered." He briefly considered her face. "Looks like the same old face to me."

She bared her teeth in a grin. "Flatterer."

"I know better than to flatter you." His grin was as fake as hers. "Remember that time I told you I thought you were smarter than that friend of yours... what was her name?"

"Tiffany."

"You filled my bed with ice cubes," Doug said.

"Even then I recognized when I was being patronized. Every time Tiffany came over, you and David fell all over yourselves entertaining her. It was miserably obvious that a pretty face, nice teeth and long blond waves had it over a mop of curls and a mouth full of metal, brains or no brains."

"College boys are driven by their hormones."

"You weren't a college boy then. You were twenty-three."

"Seven years ago." He tipped her chin up. "And the leading tomboy of Summit County metamorphosed into this. Who would have guessed that a rusty mop would turn into this glorious mane?" He rubbed his thumb across her lower lip. "No more metal either."

Samantha jerked her head from his grasp. "What do you want? Whenever you pretend to be nice, I know you're softening me up for a favor."

Doug's lips twitched in amusement. "Ever suspicious. The changes are all cosmetic, aren't they? Two years in Europe have added a certain gloss, but inside you're the same old Sam."

"And what was wrong with the old Sam?"

"She was a pest, a pain in the neck, a brat."

"Ah, we're back to the kind of flattery from you that I recognize," she said.

Doug's hands encircled her throat, his thumbs tracing her chin line. "You're still a pain in the neck, but with a difference. Your smart-mouthed insolence used to tempt me to wash out your mouth with soap. Now it tempts me to do something quite different with your mouth."

Breathing was difficult. Her pulse beat frantically to escape the pressure of his palms. "I suggest you fight temptation."

"I can't remember the last time I followed a suggestion of yours, but I doubt if it was in this lifetime." The smile that curved his lips failed to reach his eyes.

"I wouldn't brag about it," she said breathlessly. "Remember how many times ignoring my suggestions got you in trouble? Like the time you insisted on pulling off the road to turn around and got stuck, or the time you thought you could land that trout without a net, or the time I told you the perfume you bought your girl-friend stank, or the time——"

Doug pressed his hand over her mouth. "Enough. You've convinced me. Last night must have softened my brain if I could consider for even a second that those lips looked soft and sweet. I'd rather kiss a wet fish."

"I always said that some of those blondes you dated were all wet." She turned at the sound of her name.

David was signaling frantically from across the room. "Lynda is getting ready to toss her bouquet!"

The next thing Samantha knew she was clutching an enormous bouquet of white lilies and roses while the rest of the wedding guests applauded. David's grin and the look of satisfaction on Lynda's face told Samantha that the toss was deliberate. David had told Lynda that

Samantha and Doug were engaged. She wondered who else he'd told. She picked out her mother in the crowd. Mrs. Arden nodded in approval. Samantha closed her eyes in despair.

"If this means that you're to be the next bride, I guess Breckenridge is destined to be filled with old maids." The mocking words were spoken in her ear.

It said much for her state of mind that the best she could muster in response to Doug's jibe was a weak glare.

Hours had passed and the bride and groom had long since departed on their honeymoon trip before Samantha was alone with her mother.

Mrs. Arden dropped into a chair at their kitchen table and gratefully accepted the cup of tea that Samantha handed her. "It was a beautiful wedding. My only regret is that Alan wasn't here to see David get married."

"I'd like to think that Daddy is looking down in approval," Samantha said.

Her mother smiled across the table. "You made a beautiful maid of honor. Sometimes it seems like only yesterday that you were twelve years old and Doug was teasing you and you were retaliating."

"Mother. About today..."

Mrs. Arden waved off any explanation. "It was kind of you to keep Doug occupied so he didn't think about Lynda. I wasn't sure he would be able to cope."

Samantha gasped. "Did Doug tell you? Anyway, I didn't do it for him."

"I know. It's always been David with you. You were so crazy about your father, and after he died you substituted David for him. Then Doug came along and you resented sharing David with him. I think Lynda was a little concerned that you'd resent her. I'm glad you like her."

"Doug says I'm spoiled rotten."

"Well, not rotten," her mother said fondly.

"Mother! You're supposed to be on my side."

A brisk knock on the door preceded Doug's arrival. "I knew you'd be sitting out here in the kitchen talking over the day."

"As we always did when you and David came home from college," Mrs. Arden said.

Doug poured himself a cup of tea. "It went well, and our newlyweds should be halfway to Hawaii now."

Mrs. Arden caught him as he passed her chair and gave him a swift hug. "Thank you."

Doug patted her shoulder and sat down. "You're welcome. What for?"

"For not spoiling David's day."

Doug choked on his tea. "Good Lord! You, too? I should have known that Sam would have to broadcast to the whole town that Lynda dumped me for David. She never could pass up an opportunity to make me look like a fool."

"Don't blame Sammie. Give me some credit," Mrs. Arden said. "After twelve years, I know you pretty well. I watched you size up Lynda the moment you met her. You brought her over here to dinner as if you were showing off a prize painting. And now you feel as if David stole your favorite toy." Mrs. Arden passed Doug a plate of cookies. "You think you're wounded for life, but only your pride is hurt. You'll recover."

"I never realized before how much Samantha took after you," Doug said stiffly.

"If you mean common sense, she's got it, however little she chooses to use it." Mrs. Arden reached over and laid her hand over Doug's. "People who love you tell you the truth. If you blow this up all out of proportion, it will only make you bitter. You have a lot to offer a woman, the right woman."

"Is now when you tell me that there are other fish in the sea?" Doug asked with a crooked smile.

"I could tell you that, but..." Mrs. Arden settled back in her chair "... I don't see any need since you're practically engaged to Sammie. Remember? David told me what happened."

"Mother!" Samantha shot to her feet. "Nothing happened. David jumped to a conclusion, and it—it seemed easier to go along with him than try to explain. You know very well there's nothing between Doug and me. All that happened——"

Mrs. Arden waved Samantha back to her chair. "David told me about the medicine and the wine. I know you and Doug well enough to figure out the rest. If David hadn't suddenly got an attack of 'big brother' he'd have figured it out, too."

"So there's no reason to carry the charade any further," Doug said.

"I didn't say that," Mrs. Arden said. "I think there's every reason."

Doug gave Mrs. Arden an odd look. "It's not like you to be whimsical, Lucy."

Mrs. Arden measured him across the table, her eyes cool. "It's not whimsical for a mother to fight for her children's happiness."

"Sam and me? You must be joking."

"I was thinking more of David's happiness, although I always defend Samantha too. I don't want him to suffer because——"

"David's my best friend," Doug interrupted explosively. "You can't think . . . I'd never do anything to hurt him."

"You wouldn't mean to," Mrs. Arden said slowly. "Besides, don't you see that the reverse is also true? If David felt that he was hurting you . . . Once David gets his head out of the clouds, you think he won't notice how uncomfortable you are around his wife? What then? Will he start wondering why? Wondering what was between you and Lynda? Wondering, perhaps, about Lynda?"

"There was nothing between us. There wasn't time. Lynda met David before anything could happen. If David loves Lynda——"

"David loves Lynda. David also loves you. Are you going to make him choose between the two of you?"

Samantha clenched her fists in her lap. She'd never heard her mother speak to Doug in such a harsh manner. The air seemed to vibrate between them, while Doug was cast in stone.

"You know I'm right, Doug." Lucy Arden's voice turned pleading. "I'm not asking for anything formally announced. It would be just a small deception. I'm not asking for so much, am I?" When Doug didn't answer, she added, "It would be only for a short while. Until you've got over Lynda."

"Like a bad case of the measles?" asked Doug drily, a lopsided smile on his face. "All right. You win, Lucy. Consider me engaged to Sam."

CHAPTER THREE

"No!" Samantha burst out. "There's not enough money in the world to persuade me to marry Doug. You can't make me."

Mrs. Arden laughed. "Sammie, Sammie. I'm not asking you to marry Doug. You'd drive him to murder in the first month."

"*I'd* drive *him*! What about him driving me?"

"I'm easier to get along with," Doug said smugly.

Mrs. Arden hastily interceded. "Sammie, you're much too volatile for Doug."

"Not to mention stubborn and opinionated——"

"Don't forget too self-sufficient and intelligent." Samantha interrupted Doug's unflattering assessment. "And I refuse to reduce myself to a silly, clinging, feminine piece of fluff just to gratify your vanity."

"Feminine!" Doug hooted. "What do you know about being feminine? It takes more than long hair and a fancy dress to make a real woman."

"Children." Mrs. Arden rapped on the table with her teaspoon. "It isn't necessary to demonstrate to me how unsuited to each other you are. Sammie needs a husband who will appreciate her good qualities and not try to mold her into someone she's not. As for Doug——"

"He needs a brainless, blond bimbo who will worship at his feet and sigh lovingly into his eyes as she fetches his slippers." Samantha's eyes widened and she slapped her forehead. "That's it. That's what Doug needs to take

46

his mind off Lynda. A golden retriever." She gave him an artless smile.

Mrs. Arden's lips twitched. "You can't beat her now, Doug. I'm too tired to wipe blood off the floor."

Doug grinned at Mrs. Arden. "You know, Lucy, Sam's idea isn't so farfetched. Not a dog, of course. But training Sam to be civil and obedient. A chore of such mind-boggling dimensions that a lesser man would hesitate to attempt it, but for you, Lucy, my love, I'll shoulder the burden."

"Of all the disgusting, chauvinistic drivel...no surprise coming from someone like you, but..." Samantha turned to her mother "...I can't believe that you really expect me to subject myself to—to that just because Doug isn't adult enough to quit acting like a lovesick swan."

"Wait until you're a mother yourself, Sammie, and then you'll realize that mothers will go to almost any length to ensure their children's happiness." She stood up. "As for what I expect of you, I expect what I've always expected of you. That you'll behave with consideration for others." Mrs. Arden rested her hand on Samantha's shoulder. "You've never let me down yet. And now, bedtime for me, I'm afraid. Sammie, be sure and lock up when Doug leaves."

"He's leaving now," Samantha said as her mother left.

Doug poured himself another cup of tea. "No, he's not. You're just pouting because your mama's got your number. I'd say, Ms. Samantha Arden, that you are caught squarely on the horns of a dilemma. You can either be categorized as a selfish pig or you can be my sweetheart."

"I don't see why I should be punished just because you're acting like a big baby who had his rattle stolen."

"Doth the lady object too much?" Doug leaned back in his chair. "You're the one who crawled into bed with a unconscious man to get her kicks. How do I know what really happened?"

The outrageous insinuation took her breath away. "Of all the nasty minded... You can be sure that the next time you pass out, I—I'll leave you to your fate."

"What could be worse than the fate you got me into this time?"

"I got you into! I like that. I'm not the one who electrified the audience in the lounge last night with graphic descriptions of what he'd like to do with Lynda's breasts and stomach. I'm not the one who——"

Doug jerked her to her feet. "Shut up or I'll shut you up and you won't like how I do it. Understand?"

"You don't scare me."

"That's always been your problem. Nothing scares you. You never back down. Now you listen to me, Little Miss Tough Guy." His hand tugged the hair at the back of her head so that she was forced to look up into his face. "Like it or not, for the moment you and I are engaged. This is the first time your mother has asked a favor of me, and I intend to deliver, with or without your cooperation. David is the brother I never had, and, while you may be more than willing to gamble away his happiness just to spite me, I'm not going to let you do it."

"I wouldn't..." Samantha choked.

"I'm glad to hear that. Shall we kiss and make up?"

"No, I——" She stiffened as his hard mouth cut off her protest. Her hands grabbed his upper arms to push

him away, but instead she found herself clinging to him
as his lips sapped her resistance. Fingers, which had been
holding her head in a viselike grip, softened and wove
their way through her hair to lightly trace the whorls of
her ears. Lips, which had been hard and demanding,
gentled, pressing persuasive kisses against the corners of
her mouth until her lips trembled and parted. Doug's
hands, dropping to her shoulders, gripped tightly, pulling
her closer to his hard body. His breathing was harsh in
her ears and the heat from his body made her skin tingle.
Then he lifted his head and stood back from her, his
hands still holding her captive. Her eyes dropped before
the gleam in his, a gleam of triumph highlighted by the
fleeting hint of some other emotion.

"Well..." Doug cleared his throat. "Now I understand your reluctance to pretend to be engaged to me.
You're afraid."

Samantha's eyelids flew up. "Afraid of what?"

One finger traced her throbbing lips. "What happens
when I kiss you."

"Don't be silly." She pushed away the burning touch.
"This is the twentieth century. Women don't swoon when
they're kissed. Your technique is excellent, and naturally
I enjoy kissing you. It's good practice, if nothing else."

Doug's eyes narrowed. "Then I'll have to make sure
that you have plenty of opportunity to practice while
we're engaged."

"We're not going to be engaged. It's a silly idea and
I—— "

"Don't give a damn about David's happiness."

"That's not true!"

"Prove it."

"I don't have to prove anything to you. I'm not the one who presents an obstacle to David's happiness because I'm not man enough to be a good loser. You're a childish, selfish, immature, whining..." Running out of words, she took a deep breath. "And I dislike you heartily."

"Good. I'm glad to hear it." Doug stood at the back door, his hand on the knob. "It would be very inconvenient, not to mention embarrassing, if you fell in love with me while we were pretending to be engaged."

Samantha fought the urge to indulge herself with a king-size tantrum as the door clicked behind Doug. Leave it to him to have the last word. Smug, sanctimonious, interfering, irritating, fly-in-the-ointment Doug. She'd been home less than a month and already he'd managed to place her in an intolerable predicament. Either she did things his way or she came off a selfish beast—in contrast to his magnanimous behavior. If he was so magnanimous, he would leave Lynda alone, he would leave...leave... She shot the bolt on the back door with a loud snap. That was the answer. Doug could leave town. She looked across to his dark apartment. She'd tell him so in the morning.

"I don't see why you can't leave town. You're just being obstinate. You could go on a—a safari or something." Samantha glared across the room at Doug.

"I don't want to go on a—a safari or something," he mocked.

"Because it's my idea?"

"Because I have other plans this winter."

"That's right. You have plans to sit around and stare longingly at David's wife. True love."

Doug looked up from the slides he was sorting in his studio. "Not that I'm obliged to explain to you, but, as it happens, my photography workshops are all booked up for the next month. I can hardly cancel."

"Of course. How could I forget? I suppose the participants are all female."

"Why would you suppose any such thing?"

Curling her legs under her, she leaned back in the worn, overstuffed chair that served as Doug's only concession to visitors. "Because for some odd reason women seem to be attracted to you. If I didn't know you better, I'd have to admit that, outwardly, you're good-looking, if a woman goes for the tough, macho type." She studied him with a critical eye. "Tall, nice shoulders, a trim waist. Strong, squared-off chin, hair always hanging in your face begging a woman to brush it back. Blue-gray bedroom eyes——"

"Not bedroom eyes."

Samantha noted the dark flush of embarrassment on his cheeks with satisfaction. "Bedroom eyes. Sultry, promising eyes. And a standoffish air that challenges a woman. The famous Douglas Patton Clayborne Jr., nature photographer extraordinaire. Mom sent me that magazine piece on you. It made your life-style sound so exotic and glamorous. I could almost see you, after a long day under the blazing sun, as you strode back to your tent, the floor covered with oriental rugs, of course. Then you would sit in your tin bathtub drinking wine while some local beauty scrubbed your back."

"I don't think the magazine implied any such thing."

"No? That picture of you, with your bare back, setting up your camera to photograph a mountain lion. Did the photographer tell you to flex your muscles before he snapped the picture?''

"You must have studied the pictures very carefully.''

"Hardly. Male cheesecake doesn't appeal to me. But that's not the point. The point is——''

"That you're grasping for straws. A temporary engagement is a harmless enough deception. Why are you so opposed?''

"If you'd act like a man, no deception would be necessary.''

Doug put a box of slides in a drawer and slammed it shut. Turning, he studied her intently. "Would it interfere with a personal relationship of yours?''

"That's none of your business,'' Samantha snapped.

"Meaning it wouldn't. It probably doesn't take long for most men to discover that your cute and cuddly little exterior covers the cold heart and hard-edged soul of an Amazon.''

The snide remark hurt, but she'd never let Doug know that. "Still haven't forgiven me for always beating you at tennis, I see.'' She tapped her fingers thoughtfully on the arm of the chair. "Or is it the ski race that you're holding against me?''

"You know you cheated. Cutting across that bend instead of staying on the trail.''

"All you said was first one to the finish line wins. Nothing was said about staying on the trail.''

"I guess it was silly of me to expect you to play fair,'' Doug said. "Beating me—that's always come first with you. It doesn't matter who or what gets in your way, as long as you feel you've bested me. To hell with David or your mother or Lynda.''

Samantha rose from the chair. "You're a great one to talk. If you really cared about anyone but yourself, you'd leave. And it would be good riddance." The door slammed very satisfactorily behind her.

The guilt came later. Just why she should feel guilty was beyond Samantha's reasoning. It wasn't as if she'd embroiled Doug in her troubles. He was the one acting like a big baby and expecting her to bail him out. Well, she wasn't going to.

"By the time a man is thirty years old, he ought to be able to deal with his own problems." Doug had stayed strictly away from her all week, making it necessary that Samantha air her grievances against him to her mother as they set up the tables for the next morning's breakfast. Her mother's silence goaded Samantha into further defending herself. "And I don't see how you can think I'm selfish because I refuse to pretend to be in love with Doug. I think the whole idea is an insult to David. He won Lynda fair and square. You and Doug seem to think that, just because David finds out Doug loves Lynda, he'll assume that Lynda was unfaithful to him."

Mrs. Arden folded the napkins into the fancy designs she used on the tables. "Trust is something that married people build slowly over the years. I don't think David is going to accuse Lynda of infidelity. But I do think that Doug's broken heart could cast a shadow over their happiness."

"Doug doesn't have a heart to break. Besides, he's better off without Lynda. She's hardly his type. David was showing her the article that Doug did on the Sonoran Desert, and it was all she could do to look at the pictures of the snakes. You know what Doug went through those weeks he spent in the desert—the blistering days, the freezing nights, the bugs. I mean, I like Lynda and all that, but can you see her out in the wilds, living in a tent, and bathing in a bucket of water?''

"Don't be so blinded by Lynda's beauty that you miss her strength. If Lynda loved Doug...however, she doesn't, so the question of how she'd like the desert doesn't arise."

"I'm not the one you need to warn about being blinded by beauty." Samantha set down the plates she was carrying. "Doug always goes for women so dazzlingly beautiful that he's blind to what they're really like."

Mrs. Arden concentrated on the blue folds in front of her. "And what are they really like?"

Samantha paused in her sorting. "Have you ever seen a really beautiful rose and bent down to sniff it and there was no aroma? Doug gravitates toward women like that. Beautiful, but sort of smell-less."

Her mother laughed. "Are you saying Lynda has no smell?"

Samantha shook her head. "Lynda is an old-fashioned rose with a fabulous fragrance." She glanced across at her mother. "Perhaps that's why she prefers David over Doug?"

"Because he took time to smell the rose?"

"Laugh if you want, but yes. David made the effort to find out what Lynda is all about."

Her mother's hands stilled. "I remember the first time David brought Doug home. Outwardly Doug was polite and friendly, but I soon realized that his teasing air was a device that he used to hold people at a distance." Mrs. Arden stared off into the distance. "I often wondered if his upbringing was the cause of it. An only child with a father always busy with military matters and a mother who devoted herself to her husband's career—Doug was left to fend pretty much for himself. And I imagine that, when your father's pretty high up in rank, people try to use you. Perhaps that's why very few people are permitted access to the real Doug. He reveals very little about himself."

"Doug?" Samantha scoffed. "I can read him like an open book."

"Can you? Maybe." Mrs. Arden picked up another napkin.

"Home is the sailor, home with his wench."

"David!" Samantha flew across the room to hug her brother and his new wife. "You're back early."

"We decided we needed an extra day here to get ready to go back to work," Lynda said.

"What she really means," David added, "is that my eyeballs needed a rest from half-naked women and swaying grass skirts."

"You both look marvelous," Samantha said. An air of quiet contentment and satisfaction clung to David in spite of his peeling, sunburned nose. Lynda visibly basked in his love. "How was Hawaii?"

Mrs. Arden spoke first. "Let me call Doug and tell him you're back. Then you can tell us about it all at the same time." She left the room.

"Doug's working late," David said. "I saw lights in the studio when we passed. I thought he'd be over here." He gave Samantha an arch look.

Samantha took a deep breath and prepared to explain that David had misunderstood about her and Doug. At David's side, Lynda seemed to wilt at the mention of Doug's name and her radiant air dimmed. Suddenly

Samantha knew that she'd have to agree to her mother's and Doug's proposed deception. Swallowing hard, she gave her brother a weak smile. "I let him off the leash at least once a day," she said.

"Think of that, honey..." David draped an arm around his wife "...Doug domesticated. And by Sam, of all people. I'd have bet my last dollar that it would take a tall, cool blonde to bring Doug to heel. Wouldn't you have?"

"Maybe." Lynda's smile was fleeting. "And maybe all those blondes were simply to pass the time until Samantha returned."

David laughed. "Well, she's back now." His eyes twinkled at Samantha. "You and Doug ought to tie the knot soon. I can heartily recommend marriage as a wonderful institution."

"If that isn't just like a newlywed," Mrs. Arden said in a teasing voice, coming back into the dining room. "Trying to marry off his bachelor friends."

"So they'll all be as miserable as he is." Doug stood behind her in the doorway. "The kettle's on in the kitchen."

They all trooped after him. The next few minutes were hectic, with everyone talking at once. Questions and answers flew around the kitchen, about the trip, the hotel, the weather, the food, the island. The couple had stayed on the island of Maui, and tales of whaling villages, exotic flowers, sandy beaches and breathtaking scenery spilled forth. Sometimes it seemed to Samantha that half her life had been spent around this worn-out kitchen table talking things over with her family. David was telling an outrageous story about attempting to surf when it suddenly dawned on her that, beneath the laughter, other, less happy emotions lurked.

She studied the faces around her. David was cheerful, his arms waving in the air as he talked. Mrs. Arden was laughing at his descriptions, but Samantha noted that her mother's gaze continually strayed toward Doug. Lynda was smiling at David, adoration for him clearly evident on her face, and yet Samantha had the feeling that Lynda was uncomfortable.

Samantha turned her head. Doug had straddled the chair next to her, his arms resting on the back. She sucked in her breath. He was watching Lynda intently, his expression that of a child outside a candy store without a penny in his pocket. Samantha kicked him under the table. "You've got your fingers in the wrong cookie jar again," she muttered under cover of the others' laughter.

Doug glared at her, rubbing his shin. "One day you're going to provoke me too far."

"So you've been saying for twelve years." Taking a deep breath, she added, "If we're going to be even unofficially engaged, you may as well know right from the start: I'm not going to let myself be made a fool of while I'm doing you a favor, so quit mooning over Lynda. Furthermore, when we end this deception it's going to be clear to everyone that it was mutual. I refuse to let anyone think you jilted me."

Doug stared at her a minute before saying, "All right. Fair enough. What now?"

"How should I know? I'm not the Pied Piper of Breckenridge with amateur women photographers trailing mindlessly behind him."

Grabbing one of her bright curls, Doug twisted it around a finger. "Jealous?"

"Hardly."

"I'd be glad to give you private lessons. In photography, that is."

"No, thanks." Samantha knew the come-hither look that accompanied the low-spoken words was for the benefit of any onlookers, but she couldn't prevent the warm color that crept up her neck. "I'm not much interested in cameras."

"I was thinking more along the line of nudes."

Samantha blinked at the brazen proposal before she realized that Doug was deliberately trying to disconcert her. Lowering her eyelids demurely, she peeked up through her lashes. "And if I said yes?"

"I'd run like hell. I remember all those moves David taught you in case one of your dates had an overactive libido."

Samantha gave him a mocking look. "What about your image? The dashing photographer who wades cavalierly into danger, relentless in his quest for truth and the meaning of life."

"That article you're so fond of might have laid it on a little thick, but it never said that."

Gazing into his eyes in what she hoped was a soulful manner, she intoned, " 'Intrepid nomad, wandering the earth always seeking to learn, his skin bronzed, his muscles flapping...' " She frowned. "Surely flapping can't be right?"

Doug's mouth twisted in a reluctant grin. "Why didn't I stuff you in a gunnysack and drop you in the Blue River when I met you twelve years ago?"

"Because you couldn't catch me."

"Maybe I didn't want to catch you. Then."

Samantha's stomach plunged at the sensual tone in Doug's voice.

"Is this a private conversation or can anyone join?" David leaned down between them, his arms draped over their shoulders.

Samantha looked up in relief. Doug must have realized that David was standing there and he was acting for David's benefit. Irritated that she had been even momentarily deceived by Doug's seductive manner, she immediately felt the urge to strike back at him. "Thank goodness for big brothers," she said. "I need your advice. Doug wants to photograph me. Nude," she added as David opened his mouth. That would teach Douglas Clayborne to play his games with her.

"But, sweetheart..." Doug took her hand in his "...you know I'd still respect you in the morning." His lips twitched as Samantha looked at him in outraged disbelief. David frowned, but before he could say anything Doug added, "Since when do you need to hide behind your big brother, Sam? I thought you were capable of fighting your own battles?"

"I could take you on and win with one—no, with both hands tied behind my back," she retorted.

Doug grinned, his gaze locked with hers. "The idea has provocative possibilities."

David threw up his hands. "I'm a married man. I can't afford to get caught in the middle of a raging war between you two."

Doug laughed up at him. "I'm beginning to think a man would have to be a glutton for punishment to marry your sister."

David slapped him on his back. "Go bravely, my man."

Lynda and David left shortly thereafter, Mrs. Arden walking to the front door with them. Samantha stood up to follow them from the kitchen, but Doug blocked her way. His eyes never left her face. "What changed your mind?"

"Nothing you said. I couldn't care less what your opinion of me is."

His eyes narrowed and he moved closer to her, imprisoning her between his hard body and the wall. "Shouldn't we do something to seal our bargain?" he asked in a voice that purred.

"If we must." Giving a loud sigh to hide the suddenly quickened pace of her pulse, Samantha shut her eyes and raised her face. "Go ahead."

"Do you always shut your eyes when you shake hands?"

Her lids shot up at the amusement in his voice. "Only when I make a bargain with the devil," she said, annoyed by the laughter lurking in his eyes. She stuck out her hand.

Doug grinned. "I like your idea better." Bringing her hand up, he pressed a kiss in her palm. "You said you could use the practice."

Samantha snatched her hand back. "I meant kissing me was good practice for you. You're obviously the one who needs work on his technique or we wouldn't be in this predicament."

Doug's eyes were no longer laughing. He turned away. "Now that we've settled that, I'll say good night. I'm sure you have no more desire than I do to spend a second longer than necessary in the other's company." He closed the back door carefully behind him.

* * *

Samantha was supposed to be updating reservations, but her mind kept slipping back to the other night. At least she'd succeeded in diverting Doug. And just how long was she going to have to be the cavalry charging to the rescue each time he was in the same room with Lynda? While she admired steadfastness, Doug was going too far. She chewed on the end of her pencil. She had to take part in a deception; her mother was worried, Lynda was upset. Only David was in ignorance of Doug's feelings about Lynda. And he must be kept that way. Leave it to Doug to have a problem that affected everyone else.

Doug should pay for all the trouble he was causing, she thought, laying down the pencil and propping her chin on her hands. Doug was using her to camouflage his real feelings. What a perfect opportunity to turn the tables on him. She could be such a thorn in his side that he wouldn't have time to dwell on his lost love. And the beauty of her plan was that Doug couldn't do one thing about it. He needed her.

"When a beautiful woman smiles in just that way, I know somewhere a man is in trouble."

Samantha looked up in surprise at the gray-haired gentleman smiling at her over the counter. When had he come in? A fleeting sense of recognition tugged at her as she apologized for her inattention.

"That's okay. I could see you were busy." A grin flashed across his face. A familiar grin. "Plotting someone's downfall." There was a teasing twinkle in his blue eyes. "I have a reservation. Clayborne."

"Of course. Doug's uncle. We've been expecting you." She watched him fill out the registration form. "Montgomery D. Clayborne. Doug always called you

Uncle Ike.'' The significance of the name struck her and she swallowed a laugh. "I hope you don't have any sisters.''

He laughed. "Mother wouldn't have dared. Doug's grandfather was military through and through. Named his kids after military heroes: Douglas MacArthur, George Patton, British Field Marshal Montgomery, Dwight Eisenhower. My brother Douglas Patton is as dyed-in-the-wool military as our father, even if he did go to the Air Force Academy instead of West Point like our father and his father's father and so on before him. My other two brothers are Army, and their boys are Army and Air Force. Doug and I, we're the family black sheep.'' He carefully replaced his pen in his shirt pocket. "Doug is like a son to me.'' Not looking at Samantha, he added, "My wife was a long time dying of cancer. It wasn't a place for Doug.''

Samantha pasted a bright smile on her face. "It's nice to finally meet you. Doug has spoken of you often.''

Ike Clayborne cleared his throat and inspected her from head to foot. There was a paternal look in his eye, but she doubted if one detail escaped him. He nodded his head in satisfaction. "You must be Sam.''

"Why must I be?''

He laughed. "That nephew of mine has described you often enough. Those bouncy reddish blond curls, that heart-shaped face. Let me see, how did he put it? 'Speaking eyes and a face so expressive that even when her mouth is shut——' ''

"Which isn't often.'' Doug came down the stairs and hugged his uncle. "You old reprobate. I thought I saw you get out of that red car out front. I went to the room that Lucy is giving you, but you didn't show up. I should have known Sam was flirting with you."

His uncle pounded his back affectionately. "The other way around, my boy. What's wrong with the young men around here that a pretty girl like her is still roaming free? The high altitude must affect your brains."

"You'd better be careful, Ike," Doug warned. "Sam's so mean she could eat you for breakfast."

"Maybe your uncle is braver than you."

Ike's gaze flew from one to the other as they exchanged challenging looks. "Well, well, well," he said softly.

The significance of his uncle's words hit Doug first. "Good Lord, Ike," he said, his voice filled with revulsion. "I didn't mean Sam."

"Didn't mean me what?" Samantha asked.

Doug scowled impartially at her and his uncle. "I mentioned Lynda to him. In a weak moment."

"Lynda?" Ike inquired.

"My new sister-in-law," Samantha said.

There was a moment of constraint, and then Ike Clayborne said, "Oh, dear. That is awkward."

"More awkward than you think," Doug said savagely. "Now I'm unofficially engaged to Sam."

"Congratulations." Ike frowned. "I think."

"If it were true, which it's not, it would be condolences," Doug said.

His uncle looked thoroughly confused. "You're engaged to Samantha, but you're not engaged to her. I must be older than I thought because I don't understand one bit of this."

Samantha leaned across the counter and gave Doug's uncle a big smile. "It's this way," she began in a confiding tone of voice. "The sad truth is——"

"Shut up, Sam." Doug reached down for his uncle's bags. "Come on. I'll explain it to you. In your room." He gave Samantha a dirty look. "Without help."

Doug returned alone a few minutes later. Before Samantha could even open her mouth, he said, "I don't want to discuss it."

"Fine." She busied herself with her paperwork.

"A friend persuaded me to take his daughter's class on a fall nature walk. Lynda was the teacher."

Samantha didn't look up. "I see."

"Naturally I dumped the kids as soon as I could and dragged their teacher off to the woods so I could make mad, passionate love to her."

Samantha reacted to his impatient tone of voice rather than his words. "I thought you didn't want to discuss it." She laid down her pencil and propped her elbows on the counter, her chin resting on her fists. "Okay— I'm ready. Tell me your sad sob story. I promise to cry sympathetically in all the right places and feel almost as sorry for you as you do."

"Do you tear wings off butterflies, too?"

"I'm sorry. Was mean ol' Samantha picking on little ol' Dougie?"

Doug leaned on the counter, his face only inches from hers. "One of these days, little ol' Dougie is going to exact his revenge."

"I'm terrified," she said mockingly.

"You're not. But you should be. If there's one military strategy that I learned from my dad, it's how to rout the enemy." He inclined his head.

"Hey, fella, get your kisser away from my girl."

CHAPTER FOUR

LOOKING beyond Doug's surprised face, Samantha was blinded by the bright sunshine which poured through the open doorway, but she would have recognized the voice anywhere. "Andy! What are you doing here?"

"Looking for my favourite skiing buddy, what else?" Andy Barlowe picked Samantha up as she stepped from behind the counter and whirled her around the foyer, oblivious to Doug's narrowed gaze. "I told you I'd see ya soon, babe."

"Put me down," she said breathlessly, "you crazy lunatic."

"First a big kiss so I'll know how much you missed me."

"No kiss and I didn't miss you one bit," she said. When he moved to pick her up again, she yielded. "All right. I missed you a teensy bit." Granting him an opening was a mistake. Andy swept her into his arms, managing to kiss her thoroughly in spite of her struggles. Samantha finally emerged from his gigantic bear hug, more than slightly disheveled.

"Well," Doug drawled, as he leaned on the counter, "no wonder you were so reluctant to become engaged to me."

"You're engaged?" Andy gave her a hurt look.

"No," Samantha said. "Yes. It's complicated." She glared at Doug. "Aren't you late for something?"

"Nope. I'm going to lunch with Ike."

"Here I am, my boy." Ike Clayborne's voice boomed down the stairs ahead of him. "Sorry to keep you waiting."

"No problem," Doug said. "Sam was just getting ready to introduce me to her friend."

"Sam was not," she retorted.

Andy extended his hand to Doug's uncle. "Andy Barlowe."

Ike shook his hand and introduced himself and Doug before asking, "You bear a remarkable resemblance to Stephen Barlowe of Barlowe Enterprises—any relation?"

Andy nodded. "He's my father. To his everlasting shame." His grin was contagious. "I leave making money to Dad and Fraser, my brother. My role is to spend it."

"How do you know Sam?" Doug asked.

"What business is that of yours?" Samantha demanded.

"I'm a ski bum," Andy said. "I met Sammie on the slopes of the Jungfrau, and when she said she was working at an inn in Lauterbrunnen I moved right in."

"To the hotel," Samantha said hastily.

"Your idea, not mine," Andy said. "And, like a bad penny, here I am again. Ready to mount yet another assault on your virtue and your bed."

The front door opened, letting in another blast of cold air. A curvaceous brunette, the thrust of her full bottom lip showing her displeasure, stuck her head in. "Andy, we're starving. Hurry up!"

"Be right there, babe." As the door closed behind the woman, Andy turned back to Samantha, a rueful expression on his face. "You wouldn't want me to be lonely, would you?"

"You're hopeless," said Samantha, laughing. "Who is she? The daughter of an international industrialist, a movie star or a downhill racer?"

"You wound me. Prissy happens to be a perfectly nice girl whose parents own a condo in Vail. That's where we're staying. Less than an hour away, so I'll be back." He stared a challenge at Doug. "Tomorrow." Pulling Samantha to him, he gave her a big kiss. "I'll pick you up at eight-thirty for skiing. We can discuss this engagement of yours."

"Nine-thirty," Samantha said. A flip of his hand as he went out of the door told her that Andy had heard her.

"I can see that I've timed my visit opportunely." Ike Clayborne grinned at Samantha. "Doug never told me that the inn provided entertainment as well as breakfast." Glancing at Doug, he said, "I'll wait for you in the car, my boy."

The door had barely shut behind his uncle before Doug pounced. "It seems that you were learning more in Switzerland than the hotel business."

"I wasn't living in a convent, if that's what you mean, not that it's any of your business."

"I don't know. As your *de facto* fiancé——"

"Oh, no. You start trying to push your weight around and I won't be your fiancée, *de facto* or otherwise. Just remember," Samantha said, "I'm only playing your little game of pretend because I want to. I can withdraw at any time. It might be time to tell David the truth."

"Because of that character? Wait until your brother gets a load of the playboy hanging around his baby sister."

"I'm sure that this is going to come as quite a shock to you, but I don't happen to choose my male friends on the basis of what you or my brother think. Meanwhile..." she leaned back against the counter and nodded toward the door "...I imagine your uncle is hungry."

Doug reached over and brushed his knuckles across her cheek. "Trying to rush me off so you can worry in private?"

She drew away from his reach. "About what?"

"About what's going on between the pouting princess and your boyfriend, the rich Romeo."

"He's not my boyfriend."

"If you ask me——"

"I didn't."

"You ought to take a few lessons from pouting Prissy. I'll bet she knows how to make a man feel like a man."

"I don't want a man who's so insecure that I have to act like a feebleminded weakling to prevent him from feeling threatened."

Doug shrugged. "Just a suggestion. I thought if you really wanted this Alex character..."

"His name is Andy. As you well know. And, if I wanted him, I would have said yes the last ten times he proposed marriage. Now, if there's nothing else..."

"Nope. Just proving to myself that it still works."

She would not ask. Doug was almost at the door. She wouldn't. "All right. What still works?"

The grin he tossed over his shoulder was a masterpiece of complacency. "That I can always get you to tell me what I want to know. All I have to do is get you annoyed and ask the right questions. It's impossible for you to resist an opportunity to put me in my place."

Samantha scowled at his back as he went out of the door. Doug wouldn't know his place if it had his name tattooed on it.

Mrs. Arden came down the stairs carrying a basket of dirty linen. "I thought I heard male voices."

"You did. Doug's uncle has arrived." Samantha took the heavy basket from her mother. "Doug took him to lunch."

"That's nice. I suppose that David is joining them. When I asked Doug what his uncle did, he said he bred money. Apparently he buys low and sells high. Right now he's sniffing around Summit County for some good deals. With David's company handling condo management, David is the ideal person to help Mr. Clayborne. David's company is small, but he's a hard worker." Samantha's mother handed her some plastic bags, and they stuffed the sheets and towels into them for the laundry service.

"I'd think Doug could tell his uncle what he needed to know."

Mrs. Arden laughed. "I doubt if Mr. Clayborne would find helpful such information as the best place to photograph a colony of pikas."

"Pikas?"

"Those little animals that live up near the timberline around rock piles."

"I know what they are," Samantha said. "I was asking why Doug was photographing them."

"He was doing an article for a wildlife magazine. Ask him to show you the pictures. How he has the patience... at the slightest hint of danger, one speaks and they all run. They harvest grass and store it in little haystacks under boulders."

"You're a walking encyclopedia on pikas."

Her mother smiled. "Doug's enthusiasm can be contagious. Last summer he pitched his tent and spent weeks with a colony he found over on Hagerman Pass. Eventually they accepted his presence, and the result is marvelous photography."

Samantha fastened the last plastic bag and straightened up. "It's funny that Doug went into nature photography. I would have expected him to be a banker or a lawyer or politician."

"Why?"

She shrugged. "I don't know. I guess because he always seemed so self-assured. The type who enjoys running around giving people orders to see them jump at the sound of his voice."

Mrs. Arden shook her head. "I think you wear blinkers when it comes to Doug. Certainly he is self-assured. Enough so that he doesn't need subordinates to tell him how wonderful he is. A person has to like himself to spend as much time alone out in the field as Doug does."

"I forgot." Samantha made a face. "No one's allowed to criticize your boys."

Mrs. Arden patted her cheek. "Or my girl. I knew I could count on you to help Doug out."

"I'm not doing it for Doug. I'm doing it for David and Lynda." A scowl covered her face. "And the minute Doug tries to take advantage of my good nature, I quit."

"Samantha Arden, Doug is not the type to take advantage——"

"I don't mean that way, although I wouldn't be so sure," she added darkly. "I mean acting as if he has some kind of right to say what I do and where I go and whom I see."

Her mother gave her a quizzical look. "Do I gather that Doug has already tried something of the sort?"

"Tried, but I quickly set him straight. Andy may only be a good friend, but he's still none of Doug's business."

"Andy who?" her mother asked.

"Andy Barlowe. You met him in Lauterbrunnen last winter."

"Of course. He's a nice boy. Here, I assume, for the marvelous skiing." There was a teasing twinkle in her eyes.

"What else?" Samantha asked demurely. "He's staying with friends over at Vail."

"That's nice," her mother said. "I take it that Doug has already met Andy and didn't approve."

Samantha made a face. "He called him a playboy. Andy didn't impress Doug very much."

"Or else he did." Mrs. Arden nodded thoughtfully. "Andy's terribly attractive with that dimple in his chin. And that devil-may-care attitude coupled with his boyish grin..."

"He's a little young for you, Mother," Samantha teased.

"But not too young to cause Doug to suffer a tiny twinge of jealousy, perhaps."

"Why in the world would Doug be jealous of Andy? Lynda's so crazy about David she wouldn't notice if Andy had one head or two. If Doug was jealous of anyone, it would be David."

"You're right, of course." Her mother picked up the empty basket. "It's funny, isn't it? As much in love with Lynda as Doug claims to be, his relationship with David remains the same." Mrs. Arden paused halfway up the staircase. "You'd think Doug would be so crazy with jealousy that there would be some strain on their relationship."

"You're the one who thinks that Doug is so successful at hiding his feelings. Not that I agree with you. Every time he looks at Lynda, he gets this sappy, hungry look on his face. It's nauseating." After a short pause, she said, "I wonder what it would be like to be as beautiful as Lynda."

"Uncomfortable, I should think. Like being rich. Always wondering if someone was smitten with your looks or your money instead of the real you. In any case..." her mother smiled down at her "...you're not exactly hard on the eyes. Surely the fact that Andy pursued you halfway around the world proves that?"

Samantha didn't bother to set her mother straight. Andy's so-called pursuit merely proved that nothing attracted a man like uninterest and a talent for skiing.

Samantha studied her face critically in the mirror across from the reception desk. Her hair was too curly, her chin too sharp, her mouth too wide and her nose was just a nose. Features that hardly compared with Lynda's elegant bone structure and cool Nordic blond beauty.

"Mirror, mirror on the wall..."

The mocking words jerked her from her unflattering appraisal and she looked around in surprise as Doug came into the lobby carrying his skis. "What are you doing here?"

"Getting ready to go skiing with you and Barlowe," he said without enthusiasm. "Aren't you supposed to meet him at nine-thirty?"

"I don't remember anyone inviting you to come along."

"It must have slipped your mind."

Samantha scowled at him. If this wasn't just like Doug, interfering in her plans for no other reason than pure spitefulness. "It didn't slip my mind and you know it. I'm going skiing with Andy—just the two of us—and if you think I'm going to put up with you dogging my footsteps you're crazy."

"You don't think that, as your fiancé, I might object to your playing around with other men?"

He needn't pretend that he thought their charade gave him the right to dictate to her. "What I do is none of your business," she said. "I go where I want and with whom I want, and if you don't like it that's fine with me. I never wanted to go along with this whole pretense anyway."

"I see how it is. You've set me up beautifully. I have to give you credit—you played me along very nicely. Your touching concern for David..." Doug's eyes iced over. "Your reluctance to go along with the scheme was a clever touch. So clever I forgot who I was dealing with."

"I don't know what you're talking about."

"Don't play innocent with me. This whole scenario has the Samantha trademark. I must have been blind not to see it before. You sucker me into convincing David, along with everyone else in town, that I'm madly in love with you. Then the minute Barlowe, whom you've no doubt been expecting all along, hits town you plan to dump me as speedily and publicly as possible, scoring another point for Samantha. Unfortunately for your grand schemes, while nothing would give me greater pleasure than never setting eyes on you again, I promised your mother, and I intend to see this engagement through. With your total cooperation.''

Samantha stared at him in disbelief. ''You are absolutely the stupidest person I've ever known. Do you really think——?''

''I don't think. I know. I should have remembered the time you persuaded me to plant marigolds outside the kitchen door as a surprise for your mother. She was surprised all right. Especially since everyone but me knew she's allergic to the damn things.''

''That was nine years ago,'' she protested.

''Some things never change, do they?''

''You certainly haven't changed. You're just as obnoxious and pigheaded as you ever were. Everything always has to be done your way. Douglas Clayborne: small-time dictator. The only reason I wanted to go skiing alone with Andy was to show you that being engaged to me didn't give you the right to run my life. I have no intention of welshing on our agreement. I'll stay engaged to you until—until it kills me. And it probably will.'' She grabbed her ski jacket off its hook and picked up her skis. ''Well?'' she demanded. ''I assume you're coming.''

''Damn right I'm coming.'' He followed her out of the door. ''And you can save your righteous indignation for someone more gullible. You're not angry because I misjudged you. You're mad because I'm ruining your fun.'' Reaching for her skis, he attached them to the rack on the top of his car.

''Ruining my fun is an obsession with you.'' She slammed the car door and reached for her seat belt. The drive to the ski area was accomplished in total silence. As they walked from the parking lot, Samantha stopped and turned to make one more thing clear to Doug. "If you want to make yourself ridiculous by playing the jealous boyfriend, it's no skin off my nose, but don't expect me to explain to Andy why you're tagging along." His only response was a muffled choke of laughter. She looked up to see him looking beyond her, the grin on his face immediately informing her that, whatever amused him, the joke was at her expense. With a sinking feeling, she turned. Andy was waiting at the base of Peak Nine. Standing at his side, dressed in a form-fitting bright pink ski suit, was Prissy.

"Well, well, well," Doug said softly. "The day promises to be more entertaining than I'd anticipated."

They'd reached the waiting pair, preventing Samantha from giving Doug the answer he deserved. Instead she pasted a smile of greeting on her face. "Hi."

Andy gave her a quick kiss on the cheek. "Hi." The look he directed toward Doug held equal measures of pique and resignation. "Sammie, this is Priscilla Danvers. I didn't get a chance to introduce you two the other day." After presenting Prissy to Doug, he added, "The rest of the gang is skiing at Vail today, but Prissy felt sort of odd man out so I invited her to join us." Andy avoided Samantha's gaze.

"The more the merrier," Doug said. "Isn't that what you were just saying, Sam?"

"No." She yanked her knit cap down over her hair.

"Pay no attention to her, Prissy," Doug advised. "She's always a grouch in the morning."

Prissy looked from one to the other. "Are you two old friends or something?"

"Or something," Doug agreed. "We're engaged."

"Oh. Oh!" Prissy positively beamed at Doug. "Sam's engaged. I didn't know. That's wonderful. I mean, congratulations."

"Thank you. I'm such a lucky guy, I can't quite believe it's true." His smile glittered like a diamond from a dime store. And about as genuine, as he added, "A year ago I'd never have believed that Sam and I could possibly fall in love. You may not believe this, but she was the most spoiled brat in town. If you knew how many times I itched to shake her until her teeth fell out."

Prissy's smile faltered. "That doesn't sound very romantic."

Doug's eyes gleamed. "But that's the very essence of romance. Cupid's unexpected dart. One minute I considered Sam the world's worst obnoxious pest. The next," his voice deepened and he stared off into space, "there she was, her hair tousled from sleeping, her eyes pleading, her body half naked, her bare arms clinging to me——"

"I was wearing a coat," Samantha snapped, fighting the urge to wrap a ski pole around his neck.

Totally unrepentant, Doug laughed. "So you were."

Andy grabbed his skis from the adjacent ski rack. "Are we going to talk or ski?"

In the lift line, Doug stepped aside. "Sam, you ride up with Andy. I'm sure he wants to catch up on all your news."

Before she could argue, the chair lift scooped her up and she was being swept up the mountainside, Andy at her side. Settling back, Samantha took a deep breath. "Prissy seems nice."

"That doesn't sound as if you're madly jealous." Andy shifted his poles to one hand and rested his other arm on the back of their chair. "Tell me about this engagement of yours. There's something odd about it."

Samantha considered telling Andy the truth about her and Doug as the lift passed over one of the runs. A pair of brightly attired skiers startled a gray jay into flight at the edge of the trees, and the bird squawked raucously in protest. Andy had pursued her relentlessly in Switzerland. She liked him, but she didn't love him. Her engagement would shield her from Andy renewing his suit whereas the truth might give him false hope. "I don't know what you mean," she finally said.

"Don't you?" Andy played with a curl that dangled beneath her hat. "If this guy is so crazy about you, what's he doing back there with Prissy?"

"You heard him. He thought we might like to visit." Even to her, Doug's reason sounded suspect. Especially after he'd insisted on coming in order to give credibility to their sham engagement. And what was the point of those shameless remarks he'd made?

Their chair rocked as Andy turned around. "He's certainly keeping an eagle eye on you."

Samantha was unable to prevent a quick look backward. Even from a distance she could see the amusement on Doug's face. She should have known he was merely being perverse. She could hardly tell Andy that. "We haven't been engaged for very long," she said lamely.

Andy gave her a sceptical look, but, as the end of the lift was rushing to meet them, he said nothing. Doug and Prissy skied over to join them at the top of the run over to Peak Eight.

Ordinarily skiing was one of Samantha's favorite pastimes. A beautiful, crisp winter day combined with the triumphant use of skills honed by years of practice both exhilarated and excited her. Ordinarily. Today it was enough to set her teeth on edge. She couldn't quite pin down the cause of her irritation. That was, she could pin down the cause—Doug. What she would have been hard pressed to explain was what exactly Doug was doing that was so irritating.

On the surface, Doug's behavior was faultless. When Andy, treated to an exhibition of Doug's expert skills, appeared to be on the verge of sulking, Doug had shaken his head in open and sincere appreciation of Andy's skills. Doug's asking Andy to demonstrate how he'd approached a particularly tricky series of moguls had completely won Andy over. As for Prissy, it was obvious that she was crazy about Andy and not so crazy about the idea of Samantha as competition, but Doug diverted any potential awkwardness, treating Prissy like a kid sister, alternating teasing remarks with compliments until she forgot her imagined grievances. Andy and Prissy were soon totally charmed by Doug's flashing smiles and ready sense of humor. Samantha decided it was Doug's sense of humor that infuriated her. She had more than a sneaking suspicion, that, underneath all his ingenuous charm and artless admiration, Doug was laughing his socks off at the three of them. Reserving his deepest laughter for Samantha and her deepening sense of frustration and ill usage.

Samantha leaned on her ski poles as she caught her breath after a long, solid run. Two children skied past on an easier run that paralleled this one for a short distance. Their happy cries floated back to where she stood at the edge of the run. Rabbit tracks dotted the snow among the trees, and a squirrel chattered at them from a nearby pine. Prissy chattered as inconsequentially at her side. Clothes, Broadway plays, restaurants…the light conversation skimmed over Samantha's head as she watched Andy and Doug flashing down the run above her. Andy was the more skillful skier, but Doug had a natural grace that caught the eye.

"They make it look so easy," Prissy said. "It's like watching two movie stars. They're both so tall and good-looking. And don't you just love a man who's so beautifully masculine? So firm and lean and athletic." She shivered before turning a surprisingly intense gaze on Samantha. "They must both be glorious in bed. Which one is better?"

Samantha stared at the other woman in disbelief as Doug and Andy stopped beside them with a dashing flourish. Suddenly she'd had enough of the morning's undercurrents. "I'm going on down and saving us a table for lunch," she announced. "I'm starved." Without waiting for an answer, she pushed off with her poles.

Prissy's voice carried down to Samantha. "Samantha's a great skier, isn't she? She almost skis like a man."

Damned with faint praise, Samantha thought glumly. Her thighs seemed to grow to man-size proportions, and she felt like a lady wrestler.

They ate lunch in the large restaurant at the base of Peak Nine. Samantha could almost feel Prissy speculating every time the other woman looked at her. It was all Doug's fault. His earlier outrageous insinuations had guided Prissy's thoughts in this particular unwelcome direction.

"Now that we're all warmed up, who's for the expert runs on the North Face of Peak Nine?" Andy asked with a challenging look in Doug's direction.

"Sounds good to me," Doug promptly responded.

"Oh, I couldn't," Prissy said. "I'd be terrified. I'd rather walk around Breckenridge and do some shopping."

Andy turned to Samantha. "Count me out," she said. "I have work to do this afternoon." It was obvious to her that the men were planning some kind of macho competition and she had no intention of providing their audience.

"I thought you went skiing today," Ike Clayborne said, as he brought in a blast of frigid outside air.

"I did. This morning. Then I had things that needed to be done here."

"Oh." There was a trace of disappointment in his voice.

"Is there something I can do for you, Mr. Clayborne?"

"Call me Ike." He hesitated. "I was kind of hoping for a cup of tea after I leave my things upstairs."

"Certainly. Everything you need for tea is set out in the front parlor. You're welcome to help yourself."

Ike was back several minutes later, hovering around the front desk. "Actually," he said, "I was wondering just how busy you are. I don't like to drink alone."

Samantha couldn't help but respond to the smile that was so much like Doug's. "Actually," she confided, "I'm not that busy."

The pieces of a jigsaw puzzle were scattered on an old walnut library table in front of the fireplace, and they sat there with their tea. "I met David's wife today," Ike said, holding a piece in his hand as he studied the puzzle. "A beautiful woman. No wonder that nephew of mine was infatuated with her. We Claybornes have always had an eye for beauty," he added with a complacent air.

Samantha concentrated on the puzzle. "Saying Doug was infatuated seems to imply he didn't really love Lynda."

"As I understand it, while Douglas sat back and admired this woman's beauty from afar, David moved right in and snapped her up. That doesn't sound much as if Doug was in love to me. I sure haven't heard a clue that he fought for her."

"He and David are friends," Samantha said.

"That didn't stop your brother, did it?"

"David didn't know how Doug felt," she protested.

"Ah-ha." Ike triumphantly inserted a piece. "You might be right. I don't know all the players as well as you do. But it seems to me..." he studied another piece "...that David is the only clearheaded one of the bunch. And your mother, of course." He dropped the piece and picked up another. "I suppose she's too busy to sit and chat with her guests."

"Mother considers that one of her most important and enjoyable duties. Right now, however, she's out doing some shopping."

"Tell me a little about how your family got started in the bed-and-breakfast business."

"Grandfather Arden trained with the mountain rangers over at Camp Hale near Leadville during World War Two. After the war he brought his family out here for vacations. Then, in the late sixties, my dad and mom tired of big-city living and they moved to Breckenridge. Mom fell in love with this house so they bought it and, because it was too big for them, rented out some of the rooms and served breakfast. The ski area grew and

Breckenridge grew and the inn grew along with them. Dad discovered the second Victorian just as it was about to be torn down, and he had it moved over here and renovated." She shuffled puzzle pieces.

"Doug said your father died in a fall."

She nodded. "He was working on the roof of the new house."

"Your mother is quite a woman to keep this place going and raise two children."

"She always said she had no choice, but when I grew up I realized how tough things must have been for her." She knew the pride showed on her face as she added, "My mom's a fighter."

"She's certainly an advertisement for the claim that work keeps one young. I'd never have believed that she had two grown-up children." He grinned across the table. "Would you be insulted if I said you're as beautiful as she is, but she has a strength and character in her face that only age can give?"

"Well, I should be." She grinned back. "Most men don't take me aside to talk about my mother."

Ike laughed. "I can believe that. It's easy to see why poor Barlowe is camping on your doorstep."

"Andy can hardly be characterized as poor," she said.

"I wasn't referring to the wealth of the world." Ike gave her a shrewd glance. "We both know Barlowe is wasting his time. A man who has nothing on his mind but play would soon bore you to tears."

"You know me so well?"

"Doug and I have always been faithful correspondents," he answered obliquely, before changing the subject to her European travels. Ike was laughing at a long, involved story about one of Samantha's misadventures on a German train when Doug returned.

"So much for all the work you had to do," Doug said, with an expressive lift of his eyebrows. Walking into the room, he poured himself some tea.

Ike leaned back in his chair. "She *is* working. I informed her that entertaining me was her duty this afternoon. Where's Barlowe? Did you push him off the side of the mountain?"

"His other girlfriend was waiting when we finished up, and they headed downtown for shrimp and drinks," Doug said.

"His other girlfriend? I'll have to say this for Barlowe—he doesn't let any grass grow under his feet," Ike said. "You should take lessons from him." He chortled at the look on Doug's face before adding, "Meanwhile, don't let us keep you. I'm sure you must have things to do."

Doug set his cup down very deliberately. "If you two will excuse me..."

Ike waved him off. "Certainly, my boy, certainly."

Samantha waited until Doug had left the room before raising eyes brimming with laughter to his uncle. "Talk about living dangerously. I wouldn't have believed that Doug would tamely submit to that crack about taking lessons from Andy, much less allow anyone to brush him off like that. Tell me your secret."

"No secret. My nephew respects the wisdom of his aging relative."

She eyed him thoughtfully. "Leaving aside the issue of your age, what was the point of running Doug off?"

Ike gave her an innocent look. "I don't believe in sharing beautiful women."

It was unfortunate that Doug returned just as Samantha gave way to laughter. It was a foregone conclusion that he'd believe she was laughing at him. It was doubly unfortunate that Doug had come to call Ike to the phone, leaving Samantha alone with Doug.

"Enjoying yourself?" Doug asked sarcastically.

"Absolutely." She gave Doug a beatific smile. "I can't get over how charming your uncle is." Picking up the used tea things, she headed for the kitchen.

"As opposed to me, I suppose you mean," Doug said, following her.

Samantha stacked the dishes in the dishwasher. "Well..." she drawled out the word.

Doug shook his head. "Poor, unsuspecting Uncle Ike. If he only knew half of what I know about you. But you needn't worry. I have no intention of telling him."

"Why? Is Uncle Ike's little pet nephew afraid that Uncle Ike won't believe him?" Samantha slammed shut the dishwasher door.

"I know he wouldn't believe me. I've been witness too many times to the way you can cajole and beguile the most hardened heart into thinking you're some kind of angel." He folded his arms across his chest. "Unfortunately for you, it won't work with me."

Some temptations were not meant to be resisted. Crossing over to Doug, Samantha slowly adjusted the collar of his turtleneck sweater, peering up at him through lowered lashes. "Won't it?"

CHAPTER FIVE

"No." Doug captured Samantha's hands, holding them still against his chest. "But you're more than welcome to give it a try."

Samantha caught her breath at the gleam in his blue eyes, and then, annoyed by a strange weakness in her knees, she jerked from his grasp. He was the one who was supposed to be disconcerted, not her. "Never mind. I don't have the time to play your silly little games."

"Yes, you do." He pushed her into a chair.

"What's that supposed to mean?"

"Merely that a stunning revelation occurred to me this morning as we were skiing." He sat across from her.

"And do you plan to share this revelation?"

"Sure." Tipping back his chair, Doug gave a low laugh. "Not that you're going to like it."

"Well?" she demanded. "I'm waiting."

"I know. That's the beauty of it. My whole revelation in a nutshell."

Puzzled, Samantha frowned, at the same time wishing she dared wipe that smug, irritating grin off Doug's face. "What does waiting have to do with anything?"

"It's not the waiting. It's who you're waiting for. Me. That's how life is going to be until your mother releases us from this ridiculous charade. You, waiting to do what I say, when I say it." His grin took on Satanic overtones. "This is what I've been waiting for for twelve years. Samantha Arden in my power."

"Think again. I'm doing you the favor. That puts you in my power."

Doug shook his head. "That's where you're wrong. You're not doing this for me. You're doing it for David and Lynda and your mother. One thing I will admit about you—you're loyal and you love your family. You'd stand in front of a train to protect any one of them. Or sleep with a man——"

"We didn't sleep——"

"What did we do, then?"

"I meant, we did sleep. We didn't...what you were implying. And don't pretend you don't know what I mean. Nothing happened that night, and the only reason I stayed was because of David."

"Proving my point. If it weren't for David and the others, you wouldn't give me the time of day."

"As long as you know where you stand."

"I've always known where I stand with you. You made it clear the first time I came home with David. You treated me as if I were something that had just crawled from beneath a rock."

"Don't tell me I hurt your feelings," she said in a mocking voice.

"Actually, you did. Not that you really care. I was still young enough that I thought there was something wrong with me. I tried everything to win you over. Even bringing you presents. But you were hardly susceptible to bribery. Oh, you always thanked me civilly enough, but beneath that veneer of politeness your contempt showed. I grew to hate having you around because I could always tell that you were measuring me and I was coming up short."

"Poor, insecure little Dougie." She might have succumbed to guilt over his pathetic confession if it weren't for the memory of the insulting popularity book. "How could I have failed to be grateful for all those sweet, lacy socks and dainty hair bows? They were obviously so appropriate for climbing trees and going fishing."

"You mean I'd have had better luck if I'd brought you a fishing lure?"

Samantha looked coldly across the table. "There's not enough money in the world for you to buy my liking and admiration. You were an interfering pain in the neck and you still are an interfering pain in the neck." She started to rise but Doug reached across the table and grabbed her hand.

"And I'm going to be even more of an interfering pain in the neck, because..." his fingers tightened around her wrist "...as I said, I have the power." Dropping her hand, he studied her, his eyes glittering with malevolent humor. "And I intend to wield it. For years I've restrained myself. Keeping on your mother's good side always seemed more important than seeing that you got what was coming to you. Now I've changed my mind. Besides, Lucy isn't blind. She knows what an incorrigible brat you are."

The very calmness of Doug's voice filled her with foreboding, and Samantha burrowed into the back of the chair, rubbing her wrist, still warm from his clasp. "I'm not a——"

"Yes, you are. A reprehensible brat who storms through life demanding her own way. Your mother must weary of defending you."

"She doesn't have to..." Her voice died away as she recalled her mother's astonishing claim that she always defended Samantha.

Her abortive statement was not lost on Doug. His lips curved in a mocking smile. "I put up with you out of deference to your family, but maybe tolerance was the wrong attitude. Maybe all these years your mother has been praying that I'd do what she's never been able to do. Teach you a lesson." Stretching across the table, he imprisoned her chin in a hard grip. "We'll see just how sweet revenge can be."

Samantha swallowed hard. "Revenge?" Her voice seemed to echo hollowly in the kitchen.

"Revenge." Releasing her chin, he flicked a finger against her cheek. "For over a decade's worth of slights and slurs. I'm afraid that it's going to take a great deal of...shall we say, cooperation?...on your part to make amends."

Her cheek stung. "You're crazy if you think that I'll allow you to——"

"You'll allow it, all right. You have no alternative. We wouldn't want anything to mar David's and Lynda's marital bliss, would we? Not to mention making your mother unhappy." His voice was bitter.

"You're angry because we put David's happiness before yours, aren't you? Didn't we feel sorry enough for you?"

Doug's face paled. "This has nothing to do with my feelings about Lynda."

"I can't believe what I'm hearing. It has everything to do with them and your inability to cope with unrequited love."

His eyes narrowed. "If I ever had a moment's doubt about what you deserve, that remark right there exploded it."

Samantha thrust her chair back and stood up. "Our so-called engagement is off right now."

Doug slowly shook his head. "No, it's not. You never go back on your word. You told your mother you'd do this. Just this morning you told me that you'd go through with it, if it killed you." He rose to his feet and came around the table, not stopping until he was facing her. "Remember this morning?" he asked silkily. "When you didn't want me to go skiing with you and your boyfriend. But I did, didn't I? And there wasn't anything you could do about it. That's when I realized just exactly what power this whole arrangement gives me. You can't defy me. I have you right here..." he held out his palm "... and there's nothing you can do about it." His hand curled slowly, deliberately into a tight fist.

Samantha felt as if a giant hand were squeezing her chest. "That's nothing more than blackmail." Doug grinned, a grin that did nothing to lessen her apprehension. She fought against the utter panic that threatened to overwhelm her. Doug was right. She had no choice. Not when her brother's happiness might depend on her. Not when she'd promised her mother. "I won't go to bed with you. I won't go that far," she cried. "I'll tell David the truth before I'll do that." As soon as the words were out, she knew they were a mistake. Doug's face seemed to turn into a block of solid ice before her eyes.

"I have no intention of forcing you into my bed," he bit out.

"Just publicly making a fool of me, I suppose," she said bitterly.

"No. This is a private vendetta. Just between you and me." He reached down and captured one of her curls. "I don't require public retribution. It's enough for me to know that I have power over you. To know that you know it and that you hate it. And that there's not one damned thing you can do about it." He wrapped the curl around his finger, propelling her face closer to his. "Knowing that you're squirming like a worm on a hook."

"I don't believe you. This whole mess is your fault and you're using the situation to take advantage..."

"I know. Unfair, isn't it?" His warm breath stroked her face.

"I never realized before that you were the type to bear a grudge."

"There's lots you don't know about me," he said. "And one of the first things you need to learn is when to shut up."

"I..." At the look in his eyes, she promptly swallowed the rest of her protest. Doug was daring her to argue, daring her to provoke him into action. And she knew exactly what form that action would take. He was standing too close to her, the heat from his body enveloping her. Her eyelids dropped and she concentrated on the front of his sweater. Deep burgundy with cables running up and down his body, clinging to his skin, outlining his broad chest. Her breath caught in her throat. Why didn't he say something? Do something? One of his hands rested on her shoulder; the other was still entwined in her hair.

"Instant silence." Doug chuckled. "Ah, the power of blackmail." He tipped up her chin. "I know I'll pay when this is over, but, whatever the cost, these few moments of revenge will be worth it." He dropped a quick kiss on her unresponsive lips. "David has invited us over for dinner tomorrow night—no doubt to demonstrate some of the pleasures of matrimony. I'll pick you up at six-thirty. Plan to be on your best behavior, if you have such a thing." The door closed behind him.

Samantha didn't see Doug again until he arrived to take her to dinner the next evening. In the intervening twenty-four hours her mind had frantically scrambled for a way out of the trap that Doug had forced her into. She could see none. There was no point in going to her mother— Mrs. Arden would only laugh, saying that Samantha must have misunderstood Doug's teasing. Even if her mother did question Doug, Doug would be able to convince her that Samantha was overreacting. Going to David was out of the question. The only thing she could say to him would be the truth, and if she could tell David the truth then she wouldn't be in this predicament in the first place.

There was no doubt in her mind that Doug intended to make her life a living hell. Revenge, indeed. As if all the slights and slurs over the past twelve years had originated with her. He was the one who'd intruded where he wasn't wanted. He was the one who'd ingratiated himself with her mother and brother, deceiving them as to his true character. Deceiving them so successfully that they'd never believe that he was blackmailing her.

Blackmail. An unsavory word. Into doing what? Not into his bed, he'd said. No, he wouldn't go that far. No matter how little he claimed she knew him, she did know him well enough to know that he'd never physically injure her or do anything that might make David or her mother suffer. There was only one person Doug wanted to make miserable. It was that conviction that prompted her resolve. Doug might have laid down the rules, but that didn't mean Samantha had to let him win the game.

"At least you're ready on time," was all he said as he opened the back door.

Samantha stepped out before he could come in. "I wasn't sure how much time you needed to give me my instructions for the evening." She sensed rather than saw the quick look he gave her.

"I don't trust you when you're obliging. What's up your sleeve?"

She swallowed her giggles at his apt choice of words. Looking straight ahead into the darkness, she said, "What could be? Surely you realize that you've backed me into a corner. I have no choice but to go along with whatever you want."

"Within limits, of course," Doug said dryly.

"Of course. Now, about this evening . . . do you want me to cling and sit in your lap and sigh rapturously at your every word, or am I to be coy and sneak kisses when I think no one's looking? Should I sing your praises to Lynda and thank David for bringing you home? Must I agree with your every word or am I allowed an occasional thought of my own?"

"I have a feeling that you have entirely too many thoughts of your own."

"Are you worried?"

"I always worry when you're agreeable. It's a bad omen." They pulled into the driveway of David's and Lynda's new town house. The street light was behind them, leaving Doug's face in shadow. "My only instructions..." his voice grated on the last word "...for tonight are that you behave in such a way that David and Lynda don't get suspicious that our engagement isn't genuine."

"You have my word on it."

"Whatever else can be said about you, I know your word is trustworthy."

Samantha felt a tiny twinge of guilt and then the memory of Doug's behavior on the previous day flooded back and washed away any misgivings. He deserved everything he was going to get.

David helped her off with her coat. "Aren't you afraid you'll catch double pneumonia?"

"Oh, David, you're not going to play big brother, are you? I wore this dress specially for Doug." She twirled, biting her lip to keep from laughing at the stunned look on Doug's face as he got his first glimpse of the bright coral dress. Making sure he received the full benefit of the neckline's deep V, she toyed with the gold aspen leaf dangling on its long chain. "What do you think?"

"You don't want to know," Doug said in a tight voice.

"I think it's lovely. Paris?"

Samantha turned. Lynda was standing in the kitchen doorway wearing an elegant lace apron over her lavender outfit and an anxious smile. "Basel. All I could afford in Paris was some soap." She handed Lynda a bouquet of pink carnations and then any initial awkwardness disappeared as Lynda exclaimed over the flowers.

Doug produced a bottle of wine and they paraded to the kitchen where David opened the wine and poured everyone a glass. "To married life," he proclaimed.

Samantha immediately moved to Doug's side. "Don't get pushy, brother, dear. I want to enjoy a long engagement. Everyone knows that once a woman gets married she goes way down on a man's list of priorities."

David encircled his wife's waist with his free arm. "Is that so? Do you have any complaints, Mrs. Arden?"

"No." Lynda's cheeks were bright pink from the oven. Or from embarrassment.

Doug was staring into his glass of wine. Samantha tucked her arm into his. "Obviously David is waiting to spring his true character on you. But we won't tattle on him, will we, Doug?" At his blank look, she leaned against him, squeezing his arm, and shifting her body to make sure that he had a clear view of a large expanse of skin. "Or do you think we ought to warn Lynda about David's habit of flinging his socks wherever?"

David laughed. "Do you realize what an advantage you two have, having known each other so long? No surprises."

"I hope you're wrong." Samantha followed the others into the dining room. "That sounds dreadfully dull." Doug was holding her chair and as she sat down she lightly stroked her fingers against his cheek. "Thanks, darling."

His hands came down heavily on her shoulders. "I don't think you ever need to worry about being dull." He bent down, his lips brushing her ear as he whispered. "If I were you, I'd be worried about a couple of other things, however."

Samantha merely smiled innocently at him before turning the conversation to the delicious-smelling dinner. A teasing remark about David's abortive efforts to cook pancakes one morning was followed by confessions around the table of culinary failures. Laughter flowed easily as one topic led into another. Samantha was pleased to see that Doug managed to sustain his end of the conversation without any clue that the woman he loved was married to the man presiding at the head of the table.

It wasn't until the table was being cleared for coffee and dessert that Doug was guilty of his first lapse of control. David was teasing Lynda as she reached across him for his plate. She smiled down at him, love making her gray eyes luminescent. David slowly slid his hand up and down the back of Lynda's leg. Samantha felt they had totally forgotten her and Doug's presence.

She glanced at Doug. He was watching Lynda and David with such a total lack of expression that she knew it would be a dead giveaway to Doug's true feelings if David happened to look that way. Without a second thought, Samantha whipped around the table to Doug's side. Quickly reaching for his plate, she managed to bump his full water glass. Ice-cold water cascaded into his lap. Doug shoved his chair back from the table with a sharp oath.

"Oh, no!" Snatching Doug's napkin, Samantha hastily mopped at his lap.

Doug tore the napkin from her hand. "I'll do it."

Samantha stretched across the table for her own napkin and bent down to dab at spots on Doug's pants. "I'm so sorry."

"Yeah, I'll..." His caustic remark turned into a strangled sound.

Samantha glanced up in surprise. Doug's eyes were riveted on her chest. She looked down. The bent position of her body had caused her breasts to stretch the coral knit to indecent extremes. If the neckline crept one inch lower, more than skin was going to be exposed. She had certainly succeeded in diverting Doug's attention from Lynda and David. Swallowing a nervous giggle, she leaned closer to him, swiping at some illusionary drops of water on his opposite shoulder. "There. I think that's about all."

Doug grabbed her wrists and held her away from him. "For now, maybe. I'll take care of the rest later," he added through gritted teeth.

There was no doubt in Samantha's mind that he was not referring to the spilled water. Before he could totally explode, she said, "Maybe we'd better call it an evening now so that Doug can go home and—er—dry off." From the look on his face, it was probable that the amusement she couldn't hide was only adding to Doug's fury.

The speediest leave-taking in Samantha's young life was followed by a deadly silent trip back to the inn. She wasn't, however, fooled into thinking that Doug wasn't going to discuss what had happened.

He followed her into the inn's kitchen and said in a voice which permitted no refusal, "I'll have my coffee now. While you explain why you found it necessary to douse me with ice water."

Samantha heated a mug of coffee in the microwave. "You looked as if you needed a cold shower about then. Honestly, Doug, if you can't keep your eyes off Lynda, why don't you just stay away from her for a while? You could have come up with some excuse to get out of dinner tonight. It's getting a little boring running interference for you." She handed him the mug.

Doug leaned back in his chair, his fingers curled around his mug, his eyes thoroughly inspecting her as she sat down across from him. "Boring," he said, as if testing the word. "No, I don't think tonight was exactly boring. Your dress, for example. Would you call running around town half naked boring?"

"I don't know how you can say I'm half naked. This dress even has long sleeves."

"They must have used all the fabric for them, and that's why there wasn't enough left to make the top. Not to mention the fact that it's about three sizes too small."

"I'm sorry you don't like it. I was only trying to play the part of a woman who dresses to please her man."

"I didn't say I didn't like it." Doug came around the table. "You left just one little thing out of your calculations." Hands on her shoulders lifted her from the chair and turned her to face him.

"Calculations?" The question, meant to sound innocent, was more of a guilty squeak as she saw the dark glittering in his eyes.

"I wasn't born yesterday," Doug said. "You thought that tantalizing glimpses of smooth mounds of warm flesh..." a warm finger glided down the inside edge of her neckline until it rested at the V of her dress "...and temptingly parted lips would send me screaming in the other direction. Did it ever occur to you that perhaps..." his mouth found the tip of her earlobe "...such a delectable display might have exactly the opposite effect?"

"No, I——"

"Or was it that you enjoyed what we shared the night before David's wedding?" He nipped her earlobe sharply with his teeth, and then, as she shivered, his tongue bathed the throbbing flesh.

"No," she denied breathlessly. Her eyes slowly closed as Doug pressed warm kisses under her ear, along her chin line and then down the side of her neck. She was in danger of drowning in the sensuous timbre of his voice while the fiery touch of his lips melted her bones. Her mind was a tumbled confusion of emotions. Doug was deliberately taunting her in retaliation for the evening. She knew that. And yet...

"It was hard to believe that it was tree-climbing Sam who wafted waves of scent my way each time she moved until all I wanted to do was bury my face here..." His finger traced ever-widening circles between her breasts.

Samantha grabbed his hand, pressing it motionless against her. He didn't fight her. She wondered if it was her imagination or if she could really feel her heart beating through his hand.

"I should have remembered that some things are easier to start than stop."

Samantha blinked her eyes open. "If that's an apology for attacking me, it's sadly lacking."

"You are something else," Doug said, laughing softly. "In a few more minutes I could have had you on the kitchen floor, but does that teach you to control your tongue? Of course not. And what do I have to apologize for anyway? Not for what just happened here. You were enjoying that as much as I was. No, don't even bother to try and convince me otherwise. You can't." He pushed her back down on the chair. "I think it's time we called a truce."

"Does that mean you've finally realized I'm the one in control here, not you?"

Doug snorted. "If that's your idea of control, heaven help us all. We need to call a truce, because if we continue to *fight*," he sarcastically underlined the word, "like this, your mother might be planning a shotgun wedding. Ours."

"Oh."

"Oh," he mimicked, leaning his elbows on the table across from her. "Here's the deal. I back off on my power trip and you start wearing clothes. You know what I mean," he forestalled her quick retort. "Until your mother sees reason on this, we'll be civil to each other when David and Lynda are not around and friendly when they are. You'll notice I said friendly, not teasing and seductive."

Samantha opened her eyes wide. "Why, Douglas, have you been trying to seduce me?"

"Samantha!"

She retreated at the warning in his voice. "Oh, all right. If you promise to behave, I'll polish off my wings."

"Anyone less like an angel than you are right now..."

"That's not fair. If I can't jibe at you, than you can't make cracks at me either."

A wry grin acknowledged the justice of her complaint. "Okay. We'll both swallow our remarks."

"We're more likely to swallow our tongues," Samantha said.

Doug raised his coffee mug. "To peace." Draining his mug, he set it down and stood up. "Good night."

"Doug." She glanced fleetingly at him and then concentrated on the table in front of her. "Can I ask you one question?"

"Yes, but I don't promise to answer."

"How can you be in love with Lynda and kiss me like that?"

"One has nothing to do with the other. Lynda is— Lynda. And you are wearing a very provocative dress. What usually happens when you wear it?"

"I've never had the nerve to wear it before. As you implied earlier, it's not really the style for a tree-climbing champion."

"I don't believe I implied any such thing." Doug leaned down and kissed the tip of her nose. "In any case, the tree-climbing champion has definitely filled out since her tree-climbing days."

"I still climb trees." Why she found it necessary to make that claim, Samantha didn't know.

Doug grinned. "I'm not the least bit surprised."

Samantha's thoughts were far from the steaming-hot muffins that she was removing from the baking tins. A truce. Could a war that had been waged for over a decade cease in one evening? Somehow she doubted it. All the good intentions in the world wouldn't help if Doug reverted to his normal arrogant, selfish, annoying behavior. The critical thought brought her up short. She was already anticipating disaster and blaming Doug for breaking the truce when she hadn't even seen him since their agreement last night. Which only proved how difficult it would be to break the habit of disliking him. She arranged a lacy cloth around the muffins. Doug hadn't said they had to like each other. All they had to do was avoid the type of behavior that had always set them at each other's throats in the past. Surely they were mature enough for that?

"Sammie, are you going to play with that bread all day, or are you going to let our starving guests have some?" Mrs. Arden rushed through the kitchen.

"I was hoping your mom would slow down a little since you're home," Mary said, looking up from the stove. "She doesn't look so good this morning."

Taking the hot bread to the dining room, Samantha unobtrusively studied her mother. Mary had been cooking at the inn long enough that she knew Mrs. Arden well. And if Mary said something was wrong... Her mother did look drawn this morning. Samantha moved to her mother's side. "Do you feel all right?"

"I'm just tired." Mrs. Arden rubbed the back of her neck. "I must have slept wrong last night. My shoulder is sore and my neck aches a little, that's all."

"Why don't you sit down and rest? Mary and I can handle serving breakfast."

Her mother shook her head. "Later."

Which meant not at all, if she knew her mother. Not that everything wasn't running perfectly smoothly. Samantha looked around the large dining room. Heavy carved oak furniture aligned along the walls was in keeping with the Victorian style of the house, while deep burgundy wallpaper in a tiny print provided a stunning backdrop for the botanical and bird prints that her mother collected. Porcelain plates that had been in the family for years hung over a marble-topped fireplace which glowed with a warming flame. About a dozen people were seated at small tables covered with pink cloths.

Ike Clayborne sat alone at a table for two. "I don't suppose you'd join me," he said, as Samantha set a basket of muffins on his table.

Samantha twinkled at him as an idea occurred to her. "Would you do me a favor? Invite Mother to eat with you. Without letting her know that I suggested it, and in such a way that she can't say no." At his look of inquiry, she added, "She looks tired this morning, but I can't get her to sit down and rest a minute." At his nod, she called her mother over. "Mr. Clayborne is complaining about having to breakfast alone."

Mrs. Arden laughed. "Well, we certainly can't have an unhappy guest. Why don't you join him, Sammie?"

Ike stood up and gave Mrs. Arden a bland smile. "You know, Lucy—you don't mind if I call you Lucy as my nephew does, do you?—a man in my position is used to dealing with the top. Why would I want to eat breakfast with a mere employee, even one as lovely as your daughter, when I could eat with the boss?" He pulled out the other chair. "Especially when the boss is so attractive."

"Do you always get your own way, Mr. Clayborne?" Mrs. Arden asked, sitting down.

Samantha would never have believed that it would be that simple. Carrying ham quiche hot from the oven to the tables, she was surprised to see how easily her mother was laughing and conversing with Ike Clayborne. Not that her mother wasn't always a gracious hostess, but normally she'd be sneaking peeks to make sure that all was going smoothly in the breakfast room. Samantha didn't think that her mother's lack of concern was a sign of confidence in her daughter. Coming back to the kitchen for bowls of cooked apples, Samantha told Mary of her suspicions.

"Why not? Your mom is a good-looking woman and your dad has been dead a long time. It's about time she found someone else." Mary gave her a sharp look. "Don't tell me you object."

"No, of course not." She took out the apples and then came back and reported to Mary. "I think he's talking her into spending the day with him." She absent-mindedly dried the pan that Mary handed her. "You know, I never thought of my mother as, well, as needing anyone else."

"Maybe she didn't before, but now David is married, and it won't be long before you are. Doug's been underfoot ever since David's wedding."

"Doug's always been underfoot."

Mary shook her head. "Okay, so don't tell me, but I have eyes in my head. The thought of you and Doug has crossed my mind more than once over the years."

"Me and Doug? We've always loathed each other."

"Then the day you quit loathing him I'd worry, if I were you. You'll need something to take up the slack. If you aren't careful, it could just be love."

CHAPTER SIX

LOVE. She and Doug? Mary might be the best cook in Summit County, but she wasn't much of a judge when it came to human nature. Hours later the notion was still absurd. Samantha filled the bird feeders and tossed sunflower seeds on the snow in the back yard. The air was still but brutally cold, and low clouds, heavy with snow, obscured the tops of the mountains. White flakes began to drift softly down. It was lucky that her mother wasn't around to see her outside without a coat on. The reason for her mother's absence made Samantha smile. Not only had Ike Clayborne been quick to accommodate Samantha this morning, he had somehow managed to steal Mrs. Arden away from the inn for a sight-seeing tour and lunch. Her mother needed a break. Samantha frowned. She hadn't liked her mother's wan look this morning any more than Mary had. It was time Mrs. Arden had a thorough physical checkup—if Samantha had to drag her to the doctor's office.

"Samantha!"

The impatient tone of voice told her Doug had been calling her name for some time. She looked up. He was standing on his second-floor balcony. "What do you want?"

"Stop what you're doing and wait there for me." He started back inside and then turned around. "And don't change your clothes." He disappeared from his balcony.

Three snapped-out orders in as many seconds. Only last night he'd promised to get off his power trip and here he was bossing her around, expecting her to do his bidding without so much as an explanation. She looked down at her jeans and cream-colored turtleneck. And why had he ordered her not to change? Why would she? If he was making some reference to last night... He needed to be told exactly what she thought of the way he kept his so-called truce.

"You want to take my picture?" she asked in astonishment a few minutes later as Doug set up his tripod.

He nodded. "I've been racking my brain trying to decide what to give Lucy for her birthday. Then I saw you outside in the snow and——"

"Said to yourself, that's it, I'll take a picture of the Snow Queen."

"Close enough." Holding an umbrella over his camera, he leaned down and squinted through the viewfinder. "Go ahead and finish feeding the birds."

"You're not going to take my picture right now! My hair's a mess and my makeup——"

"Looks fine."

"In case you haven't noticed, it's starting to snow out here."

"All the better. White background, white snow, white clothes, and, in the middle, your face." He went back to his camera. "Pay no attention to me."

"You mean pay no attention to the person who is standing under an umbrella remaining perfectly dry while I freeze to death out here in the middle of a blizzard?"

"Don't be such a baby. Turn your face a little to the left." He leaned over and patted her face dry with his handkerchief. "The umbrella is to keep my camera dry."

"I hope these pictures turn out spectacular enough to make my dying of double pneumonia worth while."

"Have faith. Think about something pleasant."

"I can't think of anything except hot chocolate and a hot-water bottle."

"How about the time you told the girl who phoned for me that I was at the movies with Lucy?"

"You were."

"Yeah. Only you didn't bother to explain that Lucy was your and David's mother. Sally thought I was two-timing her."

"How was I supposed to know that you dated women who were as jealous and possessive as they were suspicious?" She couldn't help the little laugh that escaped. "David told me that she threw a lamp at you when you got back to school. He thought it might make me feel repentant."

"David's trouble is he thinks you're as good as he is."

"David's a saint. I never pretended to be."

"You mean you've never managed to fool anybody," he said dryly. "Like that time you tried to convince me that there was a peeping Tom outside, and I went racing outside to catch him. Just because you wanted the chair I was in."

"But it was the most comfortable chair." She giggled. "I'd forgotten that. You were furious."

"You have a convenient memory." He was still clicking away. "Now think about kisses."

"Kisses?" She looked at him in startled confusion.

"Deep kisses, sexy kisses, kisses that knock your socks off." He gave a low laugh. "Don't tell me you don't like those kind of kisses. I'd never believe you. Not after last night."

In spite of herself, images from the previous evening flooded over her as the camera clicked.

"I see you know what I mean." After a minute he said, "Wait right here." Taking the camera, he stepped inside. He was back quickly, a large towel in his hand replacing the camera. When Samantha would have taken it, Doug backed away. "I'll do it," he said, patting her face dry.

Her face that undoubtedly was covered by a revealing blush. "I was thinking of Andy," she said. "Not last night."

Doug wrapped the towel turban-style around her hair. "Were you? You mean the very thought of Andy's kisses softens your mouth and parts your lips?" He tucked the ends of the towel into the turban and rested his hands on her shoulders. "You looked very seductive." One thumb stroked the side of her neck.

Samantha backed away. "I'm freezing."

One corner of Doug's mouth twitched. "I thought I was offering to warm you up."

"I'd prefer a cup of tea."

"Now there's a switch. You taking the safe route."

"You're the one who's worried about Mother and her shotgun."

"Lucy isn't home. And, if she were, she'd have a fit if I sent you home shivering like that." He pushed her ahead of him up the two flights of stairs to his apartment and into a plush easy chair. "Sit. I'll make the tea." Hands on the arm of the chair, he leaned down. "You needn't be afraid."

"I've never been afraid of you."

"Unfortunately." Amusement flared in Doug's eyes. "We do seem to have trouble abiding by the terms of our truce, don't we?"

"What do you mean, we? All you said was that I was supposed to wear clothes. I'm dressed."

Doug's gaze flicked over her. "Skintight jeans and a form-fitting sweater."

"Maybe you'd like me to run around in snow pants and a parka," she said tartly.

Doug's eyes darkened. "You don't want to know what I'd like." He straightened up. "I'll get your tea."

The apartment was warm. From being outside, she told herself, tugging the towel from her head and shaking out her curls. If only it were so easy to shake off the spell cast by Doug's blue eyes. Samantha leaned her head against the back of the chair. It was time she stopped deceiving herself. Her surroundings weren't warm. The heat which flooded her body was generated by an almost unbearable sexual tension that flashed between her and Doug. The fact that they disliked each other made such awareness all the more dangerous. And erotic. It had been there ever since the evening she'd put him to bed, shimmering with lethal promise beneath the surface of their most prosaic conversation. Prudence, sanity, common sense—all seemed to diminish in the face of such glittering temptation. Forbidden fruit.

Doug handed her a cup of steaming tea. "Dried off?"

"Yes. Thank you."

He dropped into a chair across from her. "See? We can be civilized in each other's company."

Her gaze fell under his penetrating stare, and she looked desperately around. There must be something safe they could talk about. A pile of gardening magazines were piled on the table beside her. "What's this? Don't tell me you're hired on to do our yard work this summer?" She held up several seed catalogs.

"Hardly. You remember Annie Seton?"

"She must be about a hundred and twenty by now."

"Not quite, but she doesn't get around as much as she used to and spends hours sitting at her window looking out. Refuses to have a television. Claims it's a modern contraption that's just a bunch of noise." Picking up a magazine, he thumbed through it until he found a loose piece of graph paper with drawings on it. "I'm designing a nature garden for her. I found an old tree root this guy was getting ready to cut up for firewood and bought it from him. I'm going to sink it here for the birds to nest in. The birdbath goes here. Some of this will take a couple of years to mature, but red flowers will bring in the hummingbirds right away. Of course, she'll have to have columbine and poppies. Thinking about the beautiful flowers that bloom up and down the main street in front of the stores in town really inspired me. I think I've talked to every successful gardener in Breckenridge." He pointed with his finger. "Here's her butterfly garden. Potentilla, cosmos, Queen Anne's lace and even a few dill plants. Some fescue grass here. I hate yards that are manicured acres of green grass that take gallons of water and say 'keep out' to wildlife. I haven't decided on the trees and shrubs yet. Something that will grow at our altitude with its short summers and hard winters and be easy maintenance and provide food for wildlife." He put down his plans with a self-conscious air. "You shouldn't have got me started."

"How did you come to be so well-acquainted with Annie?"

"Your mom sent me over there when I was looking for some information. Annie's lived around here almost since the beginning of the century. What she doesn't know about Summit County doesn't exist. And photographs." His eyes glowed. "Annie's late husband, Matthew, was quite an amateur photographer. What he managed with his limited equipment is incredible. I've been helping Annie sort and label all his pictures, and I think there's a book of some sort there. Annie could certainly use the added income."

"She must be very grateful to you."

Doug shrugged. "She's doing me the favors, not the other way around. Letting me tear up her yard and sharing Matthew's photographs with me."

"Don't sound so modest. It's very generous of you."

"And don't you sound so incredulous," he said dryly. "I do have a few redeeming qualities."

"I never said you didn't." Her animosity toward Doug had never blinded her to his good side. Even if she did have a tendency to assign ulterior motives to what she called his 'boy scout' behavior. Not caring to debate the point, she stood up. "Thank you for the tea. I'd better be getting back."

Doug set down his cup and rose with her. "Don't tell your mother about my snapping you this morning."

"I won't." She hesitated at the door. "Would you— that is, could I go with you to visit Annie some time and see the photos?"

Startled, Doug looked at her, and then his eyes probed deep as if he was searching for her soul. "I'd like that," he said slowly. Deliberately, his gaze holding hers, he brushed some stray hairs from her cheek, and then his head lowered and his mouth touched hers in a brief kiss.

Samantha bolted from his room and fled down the stairs. She was halfway across the yard between the two houses before it occurred to her how revealing her flight was. Her skin tingled, and her sweater outlined the taut tips of her breasts. She shivered. It was too cold to be outdoors without a coat. Walking in the back door of the inn, she brushed the snow from her clothing.

Edna came tearing through the door from the dining room. "Am I glad to see you. Mr. Clayborne's on the phone. Your mom's in the hospital in Vail."

Samantha picked up the telephone with shaking hands. Surely Edna was mistaken. Ike's first words dynamited that hope. Numbly she listened as he explained about their stopping beside the Blue River so that Mrs. Arden could explain the historical gold-dredging operation, her mother seeing some cans tossed beside the river and insisting on scrambling down the steep roadside to collect them and then collapsing as she climbed back up. Doug was there when Samantha hung up.

"Edna told me," he said. "Get your coat. I'll take you."

Samantha was incapable of thinking. Robot-like, she did as Doug instructed. The ride to Vail seemed an endless blur of apartments, ski slopes, red rock outcroppings and red cliffs, and then more apartments. As they exited from the highway, a magpie erupted into the sky, spreading his noisy alarm. Then Doug's car was bumping into a parking lot beside the solid red brick hospital.

Inside, a pale Ike squeezed her hands wordlessly. Doug pushed her into a chair in the waiting room. David was there almost immediately. He'd gone by the school to tell Lynda, and she was with him. Doug and his uncle conversed quietly in another corner. Samantha studied her hands as they spasmodically clenched and unclenched in her lap. Around them the hospital bustled with life. Life. She had to hang on to that thought. Doors opened and closed. Heads popped through doorways only to disappear again. In the distance a phone rang. Muted voices traveled up and down the halls.

Doug's hands covered hers, squeezing her fingers until they were still. "We're going for coffee. Want some?"

She shook her head. "I'm not thirsty." He left, and the seat beside her was taken by Lynda. Without looking, Samantha knew that a half a day spent dealing with children wouldn't have disturbed a hair on Lynda's elegant head. Lynda's perfume was an old-fashioned, comforting scent that brought Samantha's grandmother to mind. A non-threatening scent that would console a hurt and bewildered child. Lynda sat quietly, her serenity soothing to Samantha's shattered emotions. At last, Samantha roused herself to speak. "I knew she wasn't feeling well today. I should have insisted that she see her doctor."

Lynda touched her lightly on the arm. "Your mother is a grown woman. You can't blame yourself."

Doug returned and handed her a glass of water. "Drink it."

Samantha took a sip, watching as Lynda returned to David's side. The smile on her brother's face seemed to wrap Lynda with love. "I'm glad David has Lynda," she said to Doug. "He won't be alone." She meant if anything happened to their mother.

Ike sat across the room, thumbing through a magazine. The pages turned too rapidly for him to be reading. Doug took the empty glass from her hand and set it down. Then he started talking about the first time he'd come home with David. From there he recalled events of other visits. He told her about a camping trip he'd taken last autumn with her mother. Footsteps came and went down the hall, but Doug kept talking, his voice flowing smoothly over her.

"Mr. Arden?" The doctor stood in the doorway, a faint smile on his face as he looked at David.

Samantha sagged back against her chair. Doug squeezed her shoulder and then pulled her to her feet. Her mother was going to be all right.

Samantha couldn't stop shaking. Heart attack. Heart attack. The doctor's terrifying words sounded over and over again in her mind with mind-numbing repetition. Her hands fumbling with the dishes and silverware, she began blindly setting up the tables for the next morning. Her mother couldn't die and leave her all alone. She wouldn't let her. One took a mother for granted. You could go off and leave her, but when you needed her she was supposed to be there. Always. Samantha blinked back tears. What if her mother wasn't? She picked up the cloth napkins. And what did she do with these?

"Need some help?" Doug's voice came from the doorway.

She shook her head, not turning around. If she opened her mouth to speak... Only the tight clenching of her jaw was keeping her chin from wobbling.

"You can't just fold them in half and put them on the plates." Doug took the napkins from her nerveless hand. "Lucy would have a heart..." His voice trailed off, and he cleared his throat. "You know she thinks half the inn's fame comes from the fancy way she folds the napkins for breakfast. What are you trying to do? Ruin her reputation?'' Horror struck by his accusation, Samantha could only stare at him. Intent on his task, Doug continued, "Lucy always claimed that I liked this one because of my military background. It's called army stripe or regimental folds or something like that. I never can remember the names. Your mother must know dozens of them.'' He tucked the ends under and held the napkin up for her inspection. "What do you think?''

Samantha burst into tears.

"It's not that bad.''

She shook her head, averting her face, trying to stem the tears that streamed down her cheeks. But it was too late. The gates were open, and the resulting deluge could not be stopped. Doug awkwardly patted her shoulder, and Samantha flinched at his touch. "Go away,'' she said in a thickened voice.

"No.'' He dropped onto the nearest dining room chair and pulled her down onto his lap.

Samantha struggled to stand, but his arms held her prisoner. She pounded on his shoulders with her fists. "Leave me alone.'' His only response was to tighten his hold. Her resistance evaporated, and she collapsed against his chest, giving in to her emotions, her body shuddering from an outpouring of the fears that had been held in check ever since Ike's phone call. When at last she regained control, she was lying weakly in Doug's embrace, his strong arms cuddling her against his body. His shirt was wet from her tears. She sniffed loudly.

"Blow.'' He held a cloth up against her face.

Taking it from him, she meekly did as he bid. Then she realized what he'd handed her, and made a watery protest. "This is a napkin.''

He nodded.

"Not the one you folded?"

"Judging from your reaction, you didn't think much of my handiwork anyway."

"You know that's not..." She hiccuped, unable to continue.

"Your hip bones are digging into my stomach." He shifted them both on the chair. "No, that's better," he said, his grip once more tightening as she tried to rise. "Okay. Now the truth. The doctor said your mom is going to be fine. So, what was all this about?"

She gave a little shrug and crushed the napkin between her hands. "Lots of things make women cry."

He tipped up her chin. "I've known you for twelve years. You didn't cry when you broke your arm, when David left home, when you left home, when David got married...in fact, I don't think I've ever seen you cry. So what's going on?"

She lowered her eyelids. She'd never accused Doug of perspicacity, but her fears and weaknesses must be so visible in her eyes that even the dullest brain would be able to spot them. "I must look terrible."

"Your nose is red and shiny, your eyes are puffy and rimmed in red, you don't have any lipstick on...other than that, you look terrific. Now. What's the matter?"

She hiccuped again. "Nothing. Go away."

"All right." He stood up, dumping her from his lap. Only his rigid grasp around her waist kept her from falling to the floor. He walked to the door before he turned. "One last chance. Tell me or..." he glanced at his watch "...I'll call David. It's after midnight. He and Lynda probably just got to bed."

"Don't threaten me, or I'll—I'll..." She'd moved across the room and was clutching his arm, glaring up at him.

Doug laughed. "Or you'll what, short stuff?" Effortlessly he brushed away her hand. "Put my underwear in the freezer? Sew my shirts shut?"

"I'll tell David you're in love with his wife." The words were out before she could stop them.

Doug's face froze. "For a while there this morning... But you haven't changed, have you? You're still an unprincipled brat who doesn't allow ethics or morality to prevent you from getting your own way."

Samantha paled at soft-spoken words which were a deadly thrust to the heart. "That's right," she managed to say, turning away from him. Behind her, she heard Doug take a deep, frustrated breath.

"You win," he said coldly. "I won't call David." He wheeled and left the room.

Samantha's shoulders slumped in despair. She was alone but she would not cry. Doug was a stiff-necked busybody who never could keep his nose out of her affairs. What did it matter to him whether or not she cried and why? He'd made it quite clear exactly how little he thought of her. She threw the soiled napkin to the floor and eyed the stack of unfolded napkins with loathing.

"One of these days I'm going to surrender to impulse and strangle you or beat you or—or something." Doug was standing in the doorway glaring at her, his fists jammed against his hips.

"Why did you come back? Are you afraid you didn't shred my character thoroughly enough?"

He stalked over and grabbed up the napkins. Savagely he kicked the nearest chair away from the table and sat down. "I'm doing this for Lucy. Not you."

Samantha silently accepted his help. For the next few minutes the only sounds were the tinkle of dishes as

Samantha set the tables, glancing Doug's way every few seconds. The muscles in his shoulders were taut with anger, but he worked swiftly and efficiently. The tension in the air finally forced her to speak. "I'll tell Mother you helped. She'll appreciate it."

"Meaning you don't."

"I didn't say that."

"You don't have to. I know how your mind works."

"So you say." She picked up some of the folded napkins.

"I say a lot of things. Damn it—you know I didn't mean all that stuff about your ethics and morality. I know damned good and well you'd never say anything to David that might cause him pain. I'll even take back unprincipled."

"And brat?"

"Don't push your luck." He handed her the rest of the napkins. "Lucy has a couple of books that she used to learn all her folding tricks. They must be around here somewhere. If you can't find them, let me know, and I'll help you tomorrow night." He stood up.

"It's strange that you know how to do this."

"It's stranger that you don't. David does. Many a night we sat here and talked with Lucy and folded napkins."

Samantha managed a half smile. "My job was putting the dishes and silver on. I thought Mother would always be here to do the...." She closed her eyes and swallowed hard, a napkin clutched to her breast. "Mother's counting on me." The words burst from her, and then she couldn't stop talking. "I know I'll let her down. It's too much responsibility. Too many decisions. The bills. What to have Mary fix for breakfast. Keeping our guests happy. Mother shouldn't ask me. I can't do it. She has to get well. She has to come home. She has to. I'm so afraid.'' The outbreak of hysteria over, her confession seemed to hang in the air. How could she have made such an admission to Doug?

He took the napkins from her and walked around the room, placing them on the tables. She fumbled with the nearest silver, unable to face him. ''There,'' he said at last. ''Need any help with anything else?''

She shook her head, mingled embarrassment and confusion preventing her from speaking. Obviously he thought she was either a fool or a coward. Maybe both. She had to say something, and finally managed a begrudging, ''Thank you for your help.''

''You're welcome.'' Hands on her shoulders pressed her down on to a chair. ''Now you listen to me. Be quiet,'' he said as her mouth opened. ''In the first place, your mother is going to be okay. The doctor had no reason to lie to you. In the second place, you are fully capable of dealing with the inn. I said, listen. I'm not finished. In the third place, even if you weren't, what's the worst that can happen? A few things wouldn't meet your mother's standards, but, since every guest is well-aware that your mother is in the hospital, they won't be expecting perfection anyway.

''Besides, who said you had to handle everything yourself? Mary has been cooking for your mother for over nine years. You think she can't handle deciding what to fix for breakfast? I don't know how long Edna and Louise have been helping Lucy, but certainly long enough to know their jobs. David is only a few blocks away and I'm right next door. Do you believe we're so selfish that we'll totally abandon you? That's pretty damned insulting. Shut up—I'm still not done,'' he warned her. ''And finally, your mother's not going to die, but, even if she were, Lucy has been a damned good mother to you. Consider yourself lucky and quit feeling so sorry for yourself.''

"Are you through now?" Samantha asked, furious with his final thrust. Without waiting for his answer, she charged angrily, "You're an inhuman monster. You don't care if my mother dies. You don't care if the inn falls apart. You don't care how I feel. Well, let me tell you, Douglas Clayborne, I don't need Mary's help, or Edna's or Louise's. And I sure don't need your help. I could run this inn blindfolded with one hand tied behind my back.''

Doug's eyes narrowed. He grabbed her head with both hands and held it firmly while he scrutinized her face, ignoring her efforts to break free. "Now I'm through. That spineless ninny is gone, and tough old Sam is back where she belongs." He raised a mocking brow. "Do you really think you can fold napkins as well as I do with one hand tied behind your back?''

Reluctant laughter broke through her indignation. "You are an absolute... You did that on purpose. Remind me never to come to you when I want sympathy.''

"Lots of people can give you sympathy, but how many can fold your napkins?" he asked smugly. Following her from the dining room, he switched off the light. "You've had a long day and you're beat. You'd better get some sleep—tomorrow will be another long day. I'll wait up until everyone's in.''

"Everyone is in.''

"Okay. I'll lock up.''

"I can do it.''

A hand on her arm stopped her. "I know that." He led her over to the stairs and gave her a little push. "Go to bed."

On the bottom step, she turned and faced him. Her gaze dropped before his steady one, but she was obliged to speak. "Thank you."

"For locking up."

"Yes, and for..." Her voice died away, and she found herself fiddling with the points of his shirt collar.

"For folding the napkins." There was no mistaking the amusement in his voice.

She clenched her jaw in determination. Never in her life had she backed down in front of Douglas Clayborne, and she had no intention of starting now. "Thank you very much for forcing me to get a grip on myself," she said in a rush. Standing on the step, she only had to stretch a little to plant a fleeting kiss of gratitude on his mouth. He didn't move, except to loosely encircle her waist with his arms. She made herself continue. "I'm sorry if I insulted you by thinking you wouldn't help, and I'm sorry I yelled at you and called you names, and I'm sorry I bawled all over your shirt. I—I won't do it again."

"You incorrigible brat." He traced her bottom lip with his thumb. "There's that damned wobble again."

"I'm sorry, I——"

"Don't worry about it. Your contrition never lasts long."

"Of all the...!" She stiffened and pushed against his chest.

His arms tightened, refusing to allow her her freedom. "That's better. I don't want to kiss a weeping willow."

"Who cares what you——?"

His mouth cut off her indignant cry. She wanted to fight him, but her body betrayed her, the stiffening draining from her bones until she clung weakly to his solid warmth, her lips responding to his kisses. His breathing was as ragged as hers, while his scent curled around her nostrils, drawing her against the strength of his chest. The beating of his heart pounded against the tips of her breasts. Then her lips were bereft, her body chilled as he stepped back.

"Good night, Sammie." Turning her boneless body, he gave her a slight push up the stairs.

She obeyed him mindlessly, bewilderment and tangled emotions robbing her of her ability to think. Almost at the top of the staircase, she stopped and turned. He was looking up, watching her. His face told her nothing. "Why did you kiss me?" she whispered.

"I was merely channeling your thoughts into a different direction." His lips twitched. "As you did for me the night before David's wedding."

"I thought you didn't remember." Her hand gripped the banister.

"I had very pleasant dreams that night."

She frowned, puzzling over the hidden meaning of his words. When it came to her, she didn't like it. "Of all the arrogant men. You think that, just because you kissed me, I'll forget all my troubles and go to bed dreaming about you, as if I were some silly schoolgirl?"

"I know you will."

"You know no such thing," she hissed. Remembering the guests upstairs sleeping, she ran lightly down the stairs. "You're the last man on earth I'd dream about."

"That's not what your kisses say," said Doug, laughing softly. "Sweet dreams, Sammie."

Heedless of the noise, she flounced up the stairs.

CHAPTER SEVEN

"You don't look as if you slept five minutes." Doug frowned at Samantha as she dragged herself wearily down the stairs the next morning and into the kitchen to help with breakfast.

"I'm in no mood to bandy words with you," she said.

Doug pushed her into the nearest chair. "Mary, coffee, quick, or we'll have another emergency on our hands. If Sam doesn't feel like fighting..." He took the mug from the cook and handed it to Samantha.

"Thanks." She took a big gulp and choked as the coffee burned her mouth and cleared some of the cobwebs from her brain. "Not today, Doug. I don't have time. Why don't you go home?"

Doug turned to Mary. "Can you believe that she's trying to fire her best waiter?"

At his words, Samantha looked up sharply, and for the first time noticed that Doug was wearing her mother's apron. A snowy white affair of embroidery and ruffles, it looked incongruous on a man of Doug's size, especially against his blue-checked flannel shirt and blue jeans. "What in the world...?"

"I know. I'd look better in a butler's uniform, but the closest I had to that is my tux, and I was afraid it would smell of mothballs." Voices sounded in the dining room. "Sit," he said. "I can handle this. Finish your coffee."

"Is he serious?" Samantha asked Mary.

"I don't think you realize how much your mother means to Doug," Mary said. She handed Samantha a couple of glasses of juice. "He needs to help, so don't get on your high horse and run him off because you don't want to admit you could use his help."

Samantha couldn't imagine why she would need his help. One person could serve breakfast. She carried out the juice. That was the last time she carried out anything. While Doug hurried back and forth bearing plates of food, Samantha was engaged by first one guest and then another, all genuinely concerned about Mrs. Arden's condition and all wanting to deliver messages wishing her a speedy recovery. A few offered their services, but Samantha turned them down with thanks. Work would be accomplished more speedily with the guests out of her way, no matter how well-intentioned they were.

When everyone had left, Ike lingered behind. "I know you're busiest this time of day, so I'll go to the hospital and sit with your mother this morning." He grinned as Doug pulled up a chair. "I'm sure she'll enjoy hearing about the cute new waitress you've hired." He winked at Samantha before adding, "Tomorrow see if you can convince him to keep his thumb out of my scrambled eggs when he brings my plate."

Samantha started to say Doug wasn't going to help the next day when she remembered Mary's orders.

"If that were only the worst of it," Doug said in chagrin. "I brought Mr. Targen coffee when he asked for tea, and then I completely forgot to bring his tea. I saw at least four people switch plates when they thought I wasn't looking." He stretched his legs out in front of him. "Remind me to tip better the next time I eat out. Waiters are definitely underpaid."

"I think you must have spilled half the food down your front," Samantha said. "I'd better buy you a heavy-duty vinyl apron." Her lips twitched. "Without ruffles."

Doug turned to his uncle, a hurt expression on his face. "There's gratitude for you. I developed flat feet while she stood around looking cute... Which reminds me..." he pivoted on his chair to face her "...you haven't had breakfast yet."

Ike patted her hand as Doug left. "You're a good child."

"I don't mind the good, but I object to the child," Samantha said. "Anyway, what do you mean?"

"Letting Doug help."

She blushed. "I can't take credit for that. Mary made me."

"Honest, too," said Ike, laughing. He stood up as Doug returned with several steaming plates. "Are you coming with me to the hospital, Doug?"

Doug shook his head. "Tell Lucy I'll bring Sam this afternoon. This morning I'm going to teach these ladies how a bed is really made." As his uncle left, he added, "Air Force style."

Allowing Doug to serve breakfast was one thing; expecting him to make beds, another. Samantha said, "You don't have to——"

"That's what you think. Haven't you ever heard the old saying, 'When it rains, it pours'? Edna showed up this morning looking like something the cat wouldn't drag in. I sent her home in tears. The flu," he said in response to Samantha's startled look of inquiry. "She was determined not to let you down, but I pointed out that the last thing you need now is an inn full of sick people; plus if you get sick, you won't be able to visit Lucy."

"Poor Edna. She'll hate thinking she's let me down. I'll call her later." She pushed aside her plate and picked up her mug. "I've heard of hospital corners, but Air Force style?"

"A made bed that puts hospital corners to shame. My dad taught me. Blankets so tight that you can bounce a quarter off of them."

"Why would you want to?"

He grinned. "My opinion exactly. Unfortunately, my room had to pass a SAMI at least once a month from the time I was five years old. For the ignorant, that's a Saturday Morning Inspection."

"I don't know much about your family except that your father used to fly and now he's a general." She picked up her dishes and headed for the kitchen. "It seems odd that I've never met your parents."

Doug helped her load the dishwasher. "Didn't Lucy tell you? That pleasure is soon to be yours. Dad's touring a bunch of bases out west, including several facilities in Colorado Springs." Following her back into the dining room, he added, "Mom is flying in there to meet him, and they're renting a car and driving up here for several days."

Samantha stopped stripping the cloths from the tables and looked at Doug in dismay. "I don't have a reservation for them, and we're booked solid for the next few weeks."

"Don't worry. They're staying with me, although Lucy suggested that they eat breakfast over here. I hope you appreciate that I'll be debasing myself by waiting tables in front of my parents, who knew I'd never amount to anything if I didn't join the military."

"You don't have to help." She lifted a troubled face to him. "Ike said you and he were the black sheep."

"I've redeemed myself. 'My son, the famous photographer, you know,'" he quoted in a wicked caricature of parental pride. "Now..." he held his arms straight out in front of him "...lead me to the unmade beds."

"But your photography workshops?"

"Are only on the weekends this month. Forget it, kiddo," he said out of the side of his mouth, "I'm sticking to you like bubblegum to the bottom of your shoe."

"And just as annoying." Samantha forced herself to speak tartly. Doug's remarks had conjured up a picture of a pathetically spartan childhood, but she knew that he'd resent the slightest hint of pity from her.

Doug's bed-making technique turned out to be as good as he'd promised. Over the next couple of days, a routine for doing the inn's chores was established. Doug helped Samantha serve breakfast, and then he stripped and remade the beds before returning to his studio. Louise did the vacuuming and dusting, and Samantha ended up with the bathrooms.

"I'm not sure why the boss is the only one capable of cleaning toilets," she grumbled, surveying her red, chapped hands by the light of the fire burning in the fireplace.

"It's a shame that rubber gloves haven't been invented yet," Doug said, studying the jigsaw puzzle on the table in front of him. "By the way, I haven't seen your playboy pal lately."

"In case it's escaped your memory, I've been a little busy. Andy understands that I'm too tired to keep up with his hectic pace."

"So good of Barlowe to understand." Doug gave a snort of disgust. "What a prince of a guy. No doubt his understanding is enhanced by the fortunate circumstance of his having a playmate waiting in the wings to take your place."

Samantha looked up at the harsh note in Doug's voice. "I thought you rather liked Andy."

"I do. He's a fun kid. And, like a kid, irresponsible and self-centered. Did he consider slowing down his pace so you could keep up?"

"Why are you being so fierce about it?" Samantha rescued the piece that Doug was trying to force into the wrong place. "You're the one who had a fit when I went skiing with Andy. I'd think you'd be happy I can't run around with him now."

"Since when have you paid any attention to anything I thought? Besides, that was before you were exhausting yourself, working so hard here at the inn and then spending every spare minute at the hospital. You need some time off to relax."

"With Andy?" She laughed. "Andy is hardly a relaxing person. No, I'll leave him in Prissy's hands. I'm sure she's more than capable of entertaining him."

"Ah," Doug tapped a puzzle piece on the tabletop, "do I hear a slight tinge of jealous pique in your voice?"

"Don't be silly. I told you, Andy and I are just friends. In any case, I'm not the jealous type."

"Ha."

"Ha, yourself. What do you mean, 'ha'?"

"Who 'accidentally' dropped a full butter dish in the lap of that girl David brought home one time from college?"

"It *was* an accident," Samantha protested. At Doug's sceptical look, she added, "I was aiming for her cleavage. And it wasn't jealousy. I simply didn't want my brother dating a loose woman."

"Or any other woman," Doug said dryly.

"Besides, that was years ago. I didn't do anything to sabotage his relationship with Lynda."

"You didn't know anything about his relationship with Lynda until it was too late."

"Well, I still wouldn't have. And I can prove it. Look at all I've been through trying to ensure that no one else..." she gave him a pointed look "...messes it up either."

"You should have been a boxer. That's a hell of a jab you have."

"You started it," she insisted childishly.

"Now what are you two fighting about?"

They both looked up in surprise. Ike Clayborne stood in the doorway. "We aren't fighting," Samantha said.

Doug shook his head. "This passes for a normal conversation with Sam. Fighting is when she throws a ripe avocado at a person for absolutely no reason at all."

"No reason! After you told David that I couldn't go on that bicycle trip with the two of you because it wouldn't look right for a girl to camp out with two guys, and then I found out the real reason was because you had invited two blond bimbos to go with you. Not only that, Mother made me clean up the whole mess, and I even had to repaint the entire wall. And it was all your fault."

"My fault." Doug turned to his uncle. "She's still mad because I ducked."

Ike chuckled. "It's a good thing that you two aren't really planning to be married. I can't imagine what your children would be like."

"You're right," Samantha said immediately. "With our luck they'd be as obnoxious as Doug and as short as me."

Doug hooted. "Any kid you gave birth to wouldn't dare arrive without being exactly what you wanted for fear you'd send him right back."

Samantha stood up. "Are you accusing me of being incapable of motherly love? I'll have you know that even if I gave birth to a miniature Douglas Clayborne, I would love that child——"

"Excessively, jealously, possessively, smothering the kid until he begged to be free. Just as you did with David."

Ike sighed. "That will teach me to open my mouth."

Samantha turned her back to Doug. "It's not your fault that your nephew is rude and judgmental and dictatorial and...and a sore loser."

"While you aren't above kicking a man when you think he's down," Doug drawled.

She turned. Doug's face was expressionless, but anger flamed in his eyes. Comprehension was immediate. "I didn't mean that," she said, knowing Doug was thinking about Lynda. "I was referring to the fact that you never could bear being bested by me, whom you consider a mere female. Avocado aside, I'll bet that any child of mine will be able to out-pitch any kid of yours any day."

"Maybe." Doug walked over to the fireplace and scattered the dying embers. "But I'll pit my kids against yours in making beds or folding napkins."

"Forget the kids. Just stay away tomorrow, and I'll make all the beds, and we'll see if anyone complains."

"Okay."

"That was too easy," she said suspiciously.

Doug grinned. "Tomorrow's Saturday. I'm teaching a nature photography workshop. But don't worry—I'll be here to serve breakfast." He gave her a two-fingered salute and left the room.

Ike waited for Samantha to turn out the lights, and then he walked up the stairs with her. "You know," he said thoughtfully, "I may have been wrong earlier. Together your genes could produce children that were strong and loyal and capable of giving their parents great joy."

They paused at the door to Ike's room, and Samantha patted him affectionately on the arm. "Can you see Doug and I ever agreeing on anything, much less something as important as raising children?"

Samantha was coming down to breakfast the next morning after a restless night of dreams peopled with squads of children all bearing Doug's face and her curly hair when Andy walked in. "You're certainly up and about early this morning," she greeted him.

"I came to say goodbye," he said.

Samantha caught the newel at the bottom of the stairs. "Goodbye?" she echoed. "Are you leaving?"

He nodded. "The skiing is great here, but you know I didn't come for that. I'd hoped that a month's absence might make your heart grow a little fonder."

"I am fond of you, Andy."

"Enough to marry me?"

She shook her head. "Fond, but not in love," she said gently. "You'll always be a dear friend."

He jammed his fists into his jacket pockets. "And if I went back to the family firm and started working?" When she was silent, he gave her a twisted smile. "Never mind. I can see the answer on your face. You still wouldn't love me."

"I'm sorry," she said, sensing his pain but unwilling to speak the words that might ease it. "Besides, you'd be miserable if you went to work to make someone else happy. You have to do what makes you happy."

"How many times have I said that exact thing to my father? He never liked hearing it any better than I do."

"I'm sorry," she repeated, "but you're not the type to settle for less than the best. You deserve a wife who's crazy about you."

Andy pulled her to him and kissed her hard. Resignation mingled with pain in his eyes when he raised his head. "*Auf Wiedersehen*, babe. If you're ever on the slopes in Europe and see a sexy old man fly by, yell hello, because it might be me."

"I'll do that," she half whispered. "Good luck to a good friend and the best skiing buddy a girl ever had."

She didn't sniff until the door closed behind him.

"Far be it from me to intrude at such a touching moment, but I thought we started serving breakfast at seven." Doug was leaning against the doorjamb between the dining room and the lobby. "Having second thoughts? According to Ike, you just kissed goodbye to a pretty big fortune."

"Thank you for pointing that out. Perhaps if I ran, I could still catch up with Andy. Far be it from me," she mimicked, "to pass up money or do anything so silly as to hold out for love."

"It's hard to picture you in love."

"Oh? Just last night you were pointing out how I loved possessively and—and all that other stuff," she said.

"That's not love. Genuine love considers the other person first, allows the loved one his freedom. You've always wanted to tie your family to you for your sake, not theirs."

Hurt and anger at his unjust words propelled her into immediate retaliation. "You're certainly the expert on allowing your loved one . . ." she gave him a saccharine smile ". . . to go free." The minute the words were out, she wished she could recall them. Why did she always let Doug get under her skin?

He pushed open the kitchen door and motioned for her to precede him. "I'd forgotten how sensitive you are to a little constructive criticism."

"Constructive criticism!" She stopped in the doorway to glare at him. "More like a battering ram, if you ask me."

"I didn't." He pushed her into the kitchen, the door swinging shut behind them.

In front of the stove, Mary shook her head. "Seems like old times with you two bickering. I didn't realize how quiet it was the past couple of years with you over in Switzerland, Sam. I'm glad you're back. Your family wanted you to do what you wanted, but they sure did miss you."

"Especially me," Doug said, picking up glasses of juice. "A little snarling early in the morning... Sam's better than a ten-mile run when it comes to getting my blood flowing." He disappeared into the dining room.

Samantha stared after him in disbelief. Doug hadn't even ripped into her for bringing up his unhappy love affair. Could it be that his pain was finally beginning to fade? Serving breakfast, she studied him surreptitiously as he bandied teasing comments with their guests. Doug had never been one to parade his emotions in public, but it seemed to her that he was more lighthearted and carefree than she'd seen him since David's wedding. The guests at the inn were obviously charmed by him as he played his waiter role to the hilt.

Belatedly she considered how much she owed him for all he'd done since her mother's heart attack. She was so used to having him around that she hadn't even considered that Doug wasn't really part of their family with the same familial obligations. His own life must be suffering while he came to her aid.

Impulsively she put her hand on his arm when he followed her into the kitchen. "I want to say thank you for all you've done to help out. I really appreciate it."

"Hold that thought for when you receive my bill."

"I'm serious. You didn't have to do all this. I know you're doing it for Mom, but she wouldn't expect you to put your life on hold while she's in the hospital."

"Damn you, Sam. One of these days..." He knocked off her hand, picked up some filled plates from Mary and stalked from the room.

"What did I say?" Samantha appealed to Mary.

Mary gave her a look of disbelief. "Were you surprised when Lynda brought you dinner last night? When she and David stayed here while you visited your mother? Surprised that they set the tables up for breakfast?"

"Well, no, but David's my brother and Lynda is his wife."

"And what's Doug? Some passing stranger?"

"Oh." Guilt flooded over her. Doug came back into the kitchen and she tried again. "I wasn't trying to hurt your feelings. I didn't mean to imply that you aren't like one of the family..."

"Of course not. You're simply astonished that someone as selfish as me would even think about helping out when people I care about are suffering a crisis."

"No! I was just trying to thank you."

"It just so happens that I don't want your thanks."

"Well, you have them anyway. And you can't give them back," she added childishly.

Giving her a cold look, Doug brushed her aside and went back into the dining room.

Samantha refused to apologize further. It wasn't her fault if Doug wouldn't let her explain what she meant. Technically he wasn't one of the family. Naturally she felt grateful to him. "Your nephew is as stubborn as a mule and as pigheaded as a—a pig," she said to Ike, slapping his waffles down in front of him.

Ike poured syrup on his food. "That's Doug. Decisive, loyal, committed, firm..."

Thwarted of an opportunity to vent her bad humor, Samantha reluctantly laughed and pushed out her bottom lip in an exaggerated pout. "Everyone always takes Doug's side."

Ike's eyes twinkled up at her. "Maybe we feel sorry for him. Aren't you the one who's always insisting that you can whip him with both hands tied behind your back?''

''Not both, just one,'' she demurred, dropping a quick kiss on the top of Ike's head. ''Thank you for reminding me that I can handle him. I must be tired this morning if I'm letting Doug get the best of me.''

''Since when is necking with the guests part of the inn's services?'' Doug asked when they were both back in the kitchen.

''What's it to you?''

''Ike happens to be my uncle. When did it dawn on you that he's a better financial prospect than Barlowe?'' The cold, censorious voice was as unexpected as a slap across the face.

Samantha felt the heat redden her cheeks. ''What a rotten thing to say.''

''Convince me I'm wrong.''

''Why should I? The more I think about it, the better the idea sounds. As you said, I've just kissed away one fortune. It would be dumb to kiss away two.''

Doug grabbed her arm. ''Come on, Sam. We both know that, whatever else you are, you're not the mercenary type.''

''And I suppose that's my cue to ask what else I am.'' She scowled up at him. ''Well, you can just forget it. I have no intention of inviting a catalog of my faults. I'm sick and tired of listening to you criticize me every time I breathe.'' She jerked her arm free of his grasp. ''Ever since I came home, you've been nothing but a pain in the neck. I'm sick and tired of you and your petty problems and your petty behavior and your—your pettiness! I wish you'd just go away and never come back.'' She stamped from the kitchen.

Doug took her at her word—on Sunday morning Samantha served breakfast alone. She excused Doug's absence to the inn's guests—and herself—by saying that he was busy with his weekend photography workshop. On Monday morning she tried to laugh off his continued absence, making up outrageous guesses as to his whereabouts.

In the kitchen, Mary refrained from comment, but the look on her face left no doubt about the direction of her thoughts. When Doug didn't show up on Tuesday morning, Mary barely looked up from the biscuits she was beating. "I only hope that he's eating breakfast," she said.

Leaving Samantha with a sudden guilty vision of Doug locked up in his apartment starving to death. "He's a grown man," she said defensively. "He ought to be able to open a box of cereal."

"Cold cereal! Is that your idea of a good breakfast?"

"Of course not," Samantha said hastily. "I just meant . . . oh, for goodness' sakes, Mary. You know he's just sitting over there pouting. He's the stubbornest person in the world."

Mary didn't turn around, all her concentration apparently on the potatoes she was frying. "Seems to me, when it comes to stubborn, Doug isn't the only one around here who could cut his nose off to spite his face."

"If you're referring to me, I don't need him. I can handle breakfast, and now that Edna's back she and Louise and I can manage the cleaning just fine." Samantha's only regret was that Doug didn't know that no one missed his bed making. At least, no one had complained.

She was glad that Doug was finally out of her hair. She certainly didn't miss him. Naturally she was lonely. Stuck in the inn by her mother's illness, she hadn't the time to join her friends for social activities. Andy had left. David and Lynda came by every day, but they were so totally wrapped up in each other that being with them was lonelier than being alone. At least Samantha was spared having to explain why Doug was never around.

Samantha dreaded her mother discovering that after all these years Samantha had finally alienated Doug to the degree that he refused to even speak to her, but all Mrs. Arden had said was, "Honestly, you two," and then she'd gone on to discuss something else. What Doug told Mrs. Arden, Samantha had no idea. He continued to visit the hospital but at times chosen to avoid Samantha. The long drive over Vail Pass to the hospital seemed longer without the comfortable bickering with Doug to pass the time. Squabbling with him had been a way to let off steam and relieve the pressure of running the inn and worrying over her mother.

By Tuesday afternoon Samantha decided that the situation had lasted long enough. What was the point in feuding with someone if you couldn't see his face when you'd scored an utterly telling shot? She'd go over to Doug's apartment and inform him that she'd had entirely enough of his pouting. Standing at his door, she squared her shoulders and told herself that, if he wasn't man enough to admit he'd been to blame for the entire mess, then she washed her hands of him. He could just eat cold cereal. What did she care? Doug opened the door and she immediately blurted out, "Mary is afraid that you're starving to death, so if you'll say you're sorry, so will I."

Doug didn't say anything for a long moment. "And if I refuse?" he finally asked, his gaze intent on her face.

Samantha's stomach sank to her toes, but then indignation came to her rescue. She'd humiliated herself by coming over here. The least he could do was appreciate her sacrifice. "Douglas Clayborne—you are the most despicable, stubbornest person I know."

"That's a hell of an apology." He opened the door wider and pulled her into his apartment.

"It wasn't meant to be an apology," she ground out through clenched teeth. "I wouldn't apologize to you if—— Oh..." The last was said in a hollow voice as Samantha belatedly registered the fact that they weren't alone.

A tall man in Doug's living room had risen at their entry. The man's military bearing and lean body, so like Doug's, proclaimed their relationship. Doug's father had the same five-o'clock shadow and the same charcoal-brown hair, only his was tinged with gray at the sides. The eyes were different, a cool gray. Doug had his mother's eyes, Samantha decided, as Doug introduced her. Even sitting, his mother was elegant and well groomed. Samantha felt shabby in her jeans and sweatshirt, her lips bare of lipstick. She brushed her tousled hair back from her face. "I'm sorry. I didn't mean to intrude. I didn't realize that your parents had arrived."

Doug grinned at his parents. "The apology's for you. Sam thinks she entitled to burst into my life whenever she feels like it."

Doug's sarcastic comment mortified Samantha, but she wasn't about to give him the satisfaction of seeing her make an even bigger fool of herself by disputing it. Not in front of his parents. Not in front of two people who looked so cool and self-possessed that Samantha doubted they'd ever given rein to an emotion in their entire lives. Those extremely well-shaped eyebrows of his mother's would rise to her hairline in polite disbelief at the slightest hint of passion. Doug shoved Samantha toward a chair and she sought refuge in its overstuffed depths, praying everyone would forget her presence. Surely after ten minutes she could make her escape without being thought rude.

Deep in her own thoughts, the conversation flowed around her, and it was several minutes before Samantha caught the drift of what Doug's parents were saying. She listened in disbelief and growing anger. They were bragging about Doug's cousins, the ones that had meekly followed the family traditions. No doubt their intention was to underline the difference between those illustrious military careers and Doug's chosen path. How could parents be so blind to the merits of their own son? Samantha studied Doug from beneath lowered lashes. He was putting on a good front. No one would ever guess how much his parents' attitude must pain him. He was too proud to defend himself. Samantha straightened up. Well, she wasn't.

"Your cousin Mac was just promoted early to major," General Clayborne was saying.

"He's going great guns," Doug said. "He'll be the first of this generation to make general, don't you think?"

His father nodded. "Mac Senior will just about bust a gut, he'll be so proud. And did your mother write you about Mitch? He's headed for the Pentagon."

"Did you see Doug's pictures and article about dippers in that bird magazine?" Samantha asked.

"Yes, we did," Mrs. Clayborne said. "Which reminds me," she turned to Doug. "Arnie said to tell you that there's lots of birds in Florida and that they have some great wildlife sanctuaries down there. He's flying fighters out of McDill, AFB now."

Doug laughed. "Arnie's idea of great wildlife is a blonde in a bikini."

His dad laughed with him. "Brad insists that Arnie only chases women to keep up his image. You knew that Brad is flying tankers down in Texas? My brother Billy says he dreads the day that Brad is up in the air refueling and realizes that his brother is on the other end of the boom. You remember the way Brad and Arnie have played tricks on each other all their lives?"

"Mother was so impressed with Doug's article on Colorado wildlife," Samantha said, looking at Doug's dad. "Did you see it?"

General Clayborne gave her a puzzled look. "Yes, I did."

"Speaking of Colorado," Mrs. Clayborne said to Doug, "Still thinks his next assignment might be to the Air Force Academy, and he's counting on you being available to ski with him next year."

"Of course Doug will be," Samantha said. "Doug can just drop whatever he's doing when Still commands. After all," she added disingenuously, "Doug merely takes silly little pictures, which isn't to be compared to the important things that all his cousins do."

Doug choked as both his parents looked at her in astonishment. Catching his breath, Doug turned to Samantha. "Sam, my folks have already heard my news. Now they're trying to fill me in on all the family gossip."

Samantha ignored him. "You ought to be proud that your son is doing something that benefits the whole world," Samantha said to General and Mrs. Clayborne. "Doug's photography makes people appreciate the world around them and educate them so that they take care of our world. We need more people like Doug, not more fighter pilots or army tanks."

There was a stunned silence in the room. General Clayborne spoke first. "Young lady, I don't know where you came up with the preposterous idea that Sandy and I aren't proud of our son, but it simply isn't true."

"Sam," Doug said softly, an odd expression on his face, "if I didn't know better, I'd swear that you were protecting me from my own parents."

"I don't like bullies," she said.

"Bullies!" General Clayborne turned red with anger. "Are you accusing me...?"

Mrs. Clayborne put her hand on her husband's arm. "Calm down, Pat. I'm sure there is a perfectly logical explanation for Samantha's—er—misunderstanding."

Samantha lifted her chin, fully prepared to provide the explanation. Doug pressed his hand over her mouth. "Be quiet, you little spitfire." His own mouth took on a wry expression as he looked at his father. "Blame Ike. You know how he likes to tell everyone that he and I are the black sheep of the family. Sam evidently took him seriously and appointed herself my defender." There was an enigmatic look in the eyes that studied her face.

Samantha pushed away his hand. "What about the bed making?" she demanded. "And the room inspections?"

"You mean Lucy never made you clean your room?" Doug asked.

She felt her face color. "I never had to bounce a quarter off my blankets," she said defensively.

The general roared with laughter. "Can you still do that?"

Mrs. Clayborne was looking at Samantha. "You must have thought we were some kind of monsters. I don't suppose that I was a very good mother to Doug. He always seemed so self-sufficient that I pretty much let him go his own way while he was growing up. There never seemed to be time for things like baking cookies and going with his class on field trips..." Her voice trailed off. "You had a different kind of mother, I know."

Doug moved over to his mother's chair and sat on the arm so he could hug her shoulders. "Lucy is Lucy and you're you," he said. "And I wouldn't have it any other way."

Samantha swallowed hard. "I've made a fool of myself, haven't I?" she asked in a little voice.

Mrs. Clayborne looked from Samantha to Doug and then back again. The look of distress on her face was replaced by startled comprehension, and she shook her head slowly. "No." Her warm smile embraced Samantha. "Protecting the people you love is never foolish."

CHAPTER EIGHT

SAMANTHA looked at Doug's mother in horror. Mrs. Clayborne thought she was in love with Doug. "I don't... I mean..." She looked helplessly at Doug.

Doug gave her a sardonic grin before explaining to his mother, "Sam will go to any lengths to protect the members of her family. The other day she told me I was like one of the family. Which means she considers the right to criticize and harass me exclusively hers."

Unable to bear the amused mockery on Doug's face, Samantha mumbled an excuse and hastily left Doug's apartment. How could she have leapt to Doug's defense that way? No wonder his mother had jumped to an erroneous conclusion and his father had looked at her as if she were a foreign species and Doug... A Stellar jay high in a nearby pine squawked derisively at her as she bolted across the yard. Calling her a fool, no doubt. How could she possibly have thought that Doug needed or wanted her to fight his battles? He would never, ever let her forget her absurd defense of him. Not to mention the insult to his parents. After the bright sunlight outdoors, the dining room was dark and shadowy. And welcome. She pressed cold hands to cheeks still burning with chagrin. His parents must have been appalled by her behavior.

"I hope you don't expect me to thank you for making me look like a bawling baby in need of a guardian angel."

Samantha whirled. Doug was silhouetted in the doorway, his face in shadow. "I was trying to do you a favor," she said.

"Were you?" he asked in a low voice that vibrated with wrath. "Or does Saint Joan run around defending the world in order to compensate for the inadequacies of her own life?"

She fumbled blindly with the mail piled on the reception desk. "I should have known you wouldn't appreciate it."

"Yes. You should have."

"If that's all you came to say, then fine. You've said it. Now go away. I have work to do."

"I'll go," he said, "when I'm ready. I came here at my mother's request. She'd like you to join us for dinner tonight."

"No, thank you." How could she face his parents again?

Doug stalked across the room and grabbed her shoulders. "I'll pass on your message that you'll be happy to eat with us."

She tried to jerk free, but his grip was too strong. "I don't want to eat with you."

"I don't give a damn what you want. You've insulted my parents enough. If you refuse to go, my mother will be convinced that you despise her for being the kind of mother she was."

The humiliating knowledge that she was guilty of every charge Doug hurled at her forced her to hide behind an unwise and untrue justification. "Maybe I do."

"I wouldn't be surprised," Doug said savagely. "You've always been a narrow-minded person, ready to judge and condemn based on evidence no one but you saw."

She knew her face was as white as his. "What time shall I be ready?"

"Seven." He dropped his hands and started to leave, turning when he reached the dining-room doorway. "And Sam, behave yourself tonight. If you don't..." his gaze dropped to her lips "...I know one sure way to control you."

Color rushed back to her face. "If you mean by kissing me, I'm not worried. I know you wouldn't want your mother to get any more wrong ideas." The room suddenly felt overheated as Doug coolly measured her body. Beneath his insolent stare, her breasts seem to swell. Not daring to check, she could only glare defiantly at him.

Doug's eyes darkened and a small smile curved his lips before his intense gaze returned to her face. "It might be worth it," he said softly.

Hours later Doug's words still rang in Samantha's ears. No one would guess from his demeanor as he drove to the restaurant that he'd threatened her. A nervous spasm rippled through Samantha's insides. There had been as much seductiveness as threat in Doug's voice. She straightened her back. It wouldn't do to let Doug think that he could intimidate her.

"What a charming town this is." Mrs. Clayborne sat beside Samantha in the back seat. "I believe Doug said it was an old mining town."

"Yes. They found gold on the Blue River back in 1859. The discovery brought a flood of people seeking instant fortunes and eventually Breckenridge sprang into being. The town was spelled with an 'i' at first as it was named for the country's vice-president, John C. Breckinridge. However, Breckinridge later supported the South in the Civil War, and the town was populated with mainly Union supporters, so they changed the spelling."

"I love all these Victorian buildings along this main street."

"Me, too," Samantha said. "Luckily Breckenridge has been occupied throughout its feast-and-famine history. So many mining towns have faded away into ghost towns. Although there's lots of new construction going on downtown, many of these buildings are on the National Register of Historic Places. You must have Doug bring you down here during the day. The bright colors of the buildings are such fun, and what's inside the shops even more fun."

"Mother's only interested in the historical significance of Breckenridge," Doug interjected from the front seat.

General Clayborne snorted. "If we let Sandy loose downtown, the shopkeepers will think it's a second gold rush."

"Strictly speaking," Samantha said, "Breckenridge has already had its second gold rush." She went on to explain how, after the original gold rush had died out in the 1860s, a new gold discovery in the late 1870s had led to a second boom that had lasted through the turn of the century.

"Pat probably has the right idea," Ike said from the other side of Samantha in the back seat. "The tourist boom is probably the biggest gold rush of all."

"You won't get much argument on that," Samantha said. "The ski area opened in the early 1960s and we've been growing ever since."

Mrs. Clayborne looked out of the frosty car windows to where laughing groups moved briskly down the gaily lit street. "Such a happy, party atmosphere," she observed.

Samantha wished some of that lighthearted mood would rub off on her. Even more strongly, she wished she were somewhere, anywhere, else. Not that either General or Mrs. Clayborne gave the slightest hint that they remembered either her horrible *faux pas* this afternoon or the even more horrible conclusion that Mrs. Clayborne had drawn from it. Doug must have set them straight.

At the restaurant the *maître d'* led them across a wide expanse of green carpet to their table. Samantha was surprised to see Lynda and David already seated there, and then she realized that, of course, David knew Doug's parents. She sat down across from her brother and his wife. Ike sat at her right while General Clayborne sat on her left. Doug sat between his father and Lynda, facing his mother at the other end of the table. Under cover of the general introductions and greetings, Samantha studied Doug and Lynda. Had their greeting seemed stilted? An almost visible tension seemed to flow between the two as they appeared to avoid each other's gaze. If Doug had deliberately sat beside Lynda to prove that he was over her, it obviously was not working. Or had Doug been compelled to have Lynda as close to him as possible because he still cared so deeply for her? Samantha's heart felt as heavy as the huge beams supporting the ceiling.

"Trust an old war horse, and don't ever play poker." General Clayborne leaned over and patted Samantha's arm. "Your face would give you away every time."

"Or my mouth," Samantha said, snatched back to her social obligations. "I was terribly rude this afternoon."

"I admire a person who fights for what they believe in. Of course, wading right in without thoroughly checking out the opposition is hardly sound military strategy. Still, surprise often wins the day," General Clayborne added.

"I suppose it sounds even ruder to say I always assumed that Doug inherited his stubborn streak, his inability to compromise and his total unreasonableness from you because you're in the military."

General Clayborne laughed. "Am I to infer that you no longer believe that to be true?"

"Your son would never be as understanding and forgiving as you are." Doug's threats still fresh in her mind, Samantha glared down the table at him. "He thinks he's the only perfect person in the world." She bit down on her bottom lip. "Oh, dear. I'm doing it again—behaving badly. My mother would be mortified. Truly, when Doug's not around, I'm very well mannered."

The general leaned closer to her. "I'll tell you a secret. If you'd done nothing but mouth polite platitudes about Doug, I'd have been disappointed." At her look of surprise, he explained, "From what Doug has told us about you over the years, I'd know that you weren't letting us meet the real Samantha Arden."

Fortunately, Doug asked his father a question at that point, saving Samantha from having to respond. She could imagine the kind of things that Doug had said about her. No wonder General Clayborne thought she was behaving totally in character. For the first time, Samantha spotted a silver lining in her mother's cloud of illness. Mrs. Arden wasn't here to be appalled by her daughter's behavior.

Ike Clayborne didn't share Samantha's relief at her mother's absence. "I wish Lucy were here," he said for the third time to Doug's mother. "You'd enjoy meeting her. Maybe you could come by the hospital with me tomorrow.''

Mrs. Clayborne nodded, asking Samantha about her mother's illness. Sandy Clayborne then directed the conversation into a more general discussion about Mrs. Arden. Samantha was amused as Ike called on her frequently to endorse his praise of one or another of Mrs. Arden's fine qualities. Sandy Clayborne's questions soon bordered on a subtle inquisition. Samantha doubted if Ike would have any secrets from his sister-in-law by the end of the evening. Obviously Mrs. Clayborne suspected the same thing that Samantha suspected.

Ike's visits to the hospital were based on more than kindness and a friend helping out in time of trouble. At least, Samantha hoped that was true. Ike Clayborne was a humorous and compassionate gentleman who had tragically lost his wife. Mrs. Arden had tragically lost her husband. They deserved the happiness they could give each other. Samantha had hinted as much to her mother, but hadn't had the nerve to ask either Ike or her mother outright. It appeared that Sandy Clayborne was not going to have the same qualms. If she didn't have Breckenridge knowing every detail of Ike's plans, Samantha would be amazed.

Swallowing a grin, Samantha looked down the table to see if Doug shared her amusement. Even from a distance she could see that warm light in Doug's eyes as he listened to something that Lynda was telling him. Samantha sawed savagely at her meat. Lynda ought to remember that she was a married woman. And Doug ought to remember that Lynda was married to his best friend. The piece of meat stuck in her throat. Around her people chatted, glasses tinkled, piano music played softly. And Lynda laughed up into Doug's face. Samantha forced herself to look away.

She was facing the large windowed wall and she looked outside. The lights were on around Maggie Pond, their glow reflecting off the ice as skaters skimmed the frozen surface. A young child fell with a painful jolt that Samantha felt clear up in the restaurant. She'd gone ice-skating there once with Doug and David years ago. A set of twins, dazzling with silver-blond hair and matching powder-blue sweaters, had smiled their matching siren smiles before leading the fellows to a nearby bar. The whirls and turns that Samantha had been practicing for weeks to show them were completely forgotten. Trudging home alone, her skates slung over her shoulder, she'd blamed Doug for David's desertion. Older now, in all fairness she realized that David was as much at fault as Doug. And yet, she could never be angry with David. Her gaze returned to the two laughing down the table. It was Doug, always Doug, she thought bitterly.

After dinner, Lynda and David said their goodbyes in the parking lot and the rest of the party returned to the inn. Samantha issued a general invitation for coffee, but everyone pleaded weariness. Which was fine with her. She really wasn't in the mood to be hospitable.

As soon as Ike had disappeared up the stairs, Samantha turned to Louise. "Thanks for staying late tonight. I appreciate it."

"I didn't mind. It was Tom's lodge night. I just watched TV and set up the tables for breakfast. Nobody needed anything, but there were a few calls. I wrote down the messages."

Samantha walked the older woman to the door. "Thanks again, and drive carefully. It's starting to snow." Closing the door, she turned to see Doug leaning against the front counter. "I thought you went home with your folks."

"Thought or hoped?"

"What's that supposed to mean?"

"Come off it, Sam. A person would have to be halfway dead to miss what went on this evening. All those questions about your folks and your background. My mother couldn't have been more obvious if she were an investigator for a matchmaking bureau."

"I knew it," Samantha groaned. "Why didn't you explain to your parents this afternoon that you and I are oil and water to each other?"

"It's not me I'm talking about. It's Ike. I must have been blind. It never hit me until I saw him sitting there grinning as if he were some kind of fool."

"I thought he looked kind of cute." She checked the messages. Most were calls asking about Mrs. Arden. Just thinking of how sly her mother had been put a smile on her face. "Your mother certainly suspected something. I hope your parents don't mind."

"Mind! Of course they'll mind." Doug followed Samantha into the kitchen. "I suppose the money makes Ike look pretty attractive."

"I don't like your insinuation." She turned angrily on him. "Ike is a sweet, loving man who deserves a good wife. And if you think money is the only reason why——"

"He's fifty-eight years old."

"So what?"

"I suppose he thinks a younger woman... I find it disgusting. A man that age has no business——"

"No business what? Sleeping with a woman? Is that what you were going to say? What is the matter with you?" Her mother was only six years younger than Ike.

Both were too young to retire from the business of living. And loving. "Ike's wife died five years ago. Is he supposed to remain alone forever? I don't understand your attitude. I thought you'd be happy about it." An insidious thought struck her. "You've been expecting his money. That's it, isn't it? All these years; Ike's favorite nephew. What's the matter? Are you afraid that I might end up inheriting it?" The anger on his face made her back off, but she couldn't stop the angry words that burst forth. "Don't you dare interfere. After all my mother has done for you. You do anything to wreck this, and I warn you, I'll——"

"You'll what?" The words were an angry growl as he grabbed her arms, his fingers pressing deep into her flesh.

"Let me go." The wall behind her prevented her from backing further away from him.

Doug took immediate advantage, his hard body crowding her. Bringing up his hands, he trailed his fingers over her cheeks. "Such pretty aqua eyes. So full of innocence. Eve sharing her apple, Delilah picking up her barber shears. When did the tomboy turn into the temptress?"

Samantha could scarcely breathe, much less answer. But Doug didn't require an answer. At least, not one of words. His fingers parted her hair and then pressed deep into her scalp as he raised her to her tiptoes and covered her mouth with his. Her lips parted obediently at pressure from his demanding tongue. He tasted of wine and after-dinner mints. Desire came to life and streamed through her veins. Her fingers dug into his upper arms and at first she relished the strength of his muscles through her wool jacket. Then his jacket was a barrier to be pushed aside allowing her palms to slide over his shirt. His shirt was warm from his body and she could feel the beating of his heart. His scent surrounded her.

When Doug finally pulled his mouth from hers, her lips felt swollen and throbbing. Her whole body throbbed. And longed once more for the touch of his hands, his lips. The silence was deafening, broken only by the harsh sounds of their breathing. Knowing her eyes would betray the passion Doug had aroused, Samantha refused to look any higher than his mouth. Above a squared-off chin, lips that had been seductively compelling were firm and masculine. She fought the impulse to press kisses against the grooves that bracketed his mouth. Then the grooves deepened, and his lips thinned in annoyance before parting in a smile so filled with anger and scorn that she shook her head, denying his words before he even said them.

A thumb beneath her chin forced her face up. His eyes were so cold that they appeared more gray than blue. He inspected her face, his gaze lingering on her lips. "You must be very sure of your charms," he said, no hint of warmth in his voice.

She squeezed her eyes tightly shut. Doug hated this chemical attraction between them as much as she did. "You think I want this? That I like this?" she asked.

His thumb rubbed across her bottom lip and then trailed down her neck and across her shoulder. She sucked in a deep breath at the provocative touch. "Yes, I think you like it. Take a look." He shook her shoulders. "Look, damn you."

Her lids flew up. He was looking down, and she followed the direction of his gaze. "Oh, no." Her blouse hung open and her camisole had been tugged below her breasts to expose tight rosy nipples.

Doug swallowed her breasts with his palms. "Oh, yes," he cruelly mocked. "What would Ike think now if he came down here and saw us like this?"

She shook her head, his touch igniting the surface of her skin. She couldn't think. His words were so angry, the message so different from his kisses. Even as the harsh words somehow accused her, his hands were caressing her breasts. Wildly she wondered if he even knew what his hands were doing. "I—I don't kn-know," she finally stuttered.

"I know," Doug said furiously. "He'd think you were a tramp. And he'd leave Breckenridge and this inn so fast your head would swim. You wouldn't like that, would you? I didn't think so," he said, his voice oozing with satisfaction at the look in her eyes.

"Are you going to tell him?"

He released her and backed away as if she carried a contagious disease. "I should. That would put an end to any thoughts of marriage. Or was he even considering that? Maybe all he wanted was a mistress. Did you ever think of that?"

"No," she whispered, tugging up her camisole. "He wouldn't. Why are you being so hateful?"

"Because the whole idea sickens me." He stopped in the doorway, his back to her. "I want it called off, or I tell Ike what just happened here."

She dropped into a chair. "But why?"

He deliberately misunderstood her question. "You can give him any reason you want." He uttered a short laugh. "I don't know why I care if you save face."

"I don't care about that. It's Mother——"

"I'll see she's not hurt by it."

Samantha grabbed on to the edge of the table for support, struck by the shocking truth. "You love my mother."

Doug turned back to her. "You needn't sound so surprised. Of course I love your mother. She's like a second mother to me."

"I didn't mean that way. I meant love, like man and..." She swallowed hard at the ugly look on Doug's face as he retraced his steps into the room.

He pulled her to her feet. "I ought to slap your mouth."

"Then it's your uncle. There's something wrong with him." She flinched as he stuck his face in hers.

"The only thing wrong around here is your dirty little mind." Pushing her from him, he turned and walked away.

Samantha had had enough. "Damn you." Picking up an empty bread basket, she fired it, hitting Doug squarely in the back.

He whirled, his fists clenched. "Samantha..." He started toward her.

She retreated behind the nearest chair, clutching the front edges of her blouse together. "I want to know. Why can't my mother marry your uncle?"

Doug came to an immediate halt. "What did you say?"

"You heard me. I want you to give me one good reason why my mother isn't good enough to marry Ike."

The expression on Doug's face was one of total disbelief. "Ike and Lucy?"

"Of course, Ike and Lucy. What do you think we've been talking about?" As Doug started laughing, it suddenly dawned on Samantha exactly what Doug had been talking about. "Me!" she choked. "That's what all that nonsense about money was. You were accusing me of marrying Ike for his money. Why, you——''

Doug caught her hand and swallowed a couple of chuckles. "Ike and Lucy. That sneaky old man."

"He's not old and he's not sneaky," she said, wrenching her hand from his grasp. "You'd have seen for yourself if you spent more time paying attention to your relatives and less time mooning over another man's wife."

Doug ignored the last part of her accusation. "Are you sure?"

"I'm not positive," she admitted, "but Ike certainly acts like a man who's crazy in love."

Doug gave her a quizzical look. "How do you know about men who are crazy in love?"

She didn't have to be a genius to grasp his meaning. He doubted that any man had ever been crazy in love with her. Her emotions already raw from the tumultuous day, her anger flared easily. "How can I not know? I've been watching the sickening demonstration you've been putting on ever since David's wedding."

"I thought I behaved with total circumspection this evening."

"You don't even know the meaning of the word. It was disgusting the way you drooled all over Lynda at the dinner table. I could hardly eat my dinner, I was so nauseated."

"Maybe you're coming down with something."

"I'm not——"

"Like a bad case of jealousy."

His eyes were dark, mysterious pools that threatened to drown her in their enigmatic depths. Samantha shook her head to break their spell, whipping up her anger to shield herself. "Jealousy!" she cried. "And who am I supposed to be jealous of? Not you slobbering all over Lynda. That's disgusting."

Doug laughed, a low, provocative sound that set her muscles trembling even as it curdled her insides with trepidation. "Let's see how disgusting you really think it is."

"No," she breathed in horror.

"Why? Afraid?" Doug captured both her hands in his and held them behind her back, forcing her up against his body.

"You don't scare me." Even through her clothes, his hips scalded her body.

"Maybe it would be better for you if I did. A little pip-squeak should know better than to challenge a man of my size." His lips twitched as he studied her face. "Go ahead. Struggle."

"You'd like that, wouldn't you? Just so you could prove that you're stronger than me."

He grinned, changing his grip so that one hand secured both of hers. "I was thinking more about what it would do to your unbuttoned blouse." A finger pressed against her lips before she could speak. "Just keep your mouth shut, or I'll think your parted lips are an invitation."

"I'm not inviting you to——"

His mouth cut off her angry denial. Had that been what she really wanted? By the time Doug lifted his lips from hers, she was shaking, as much from anger as desire. It wasn't fair that Doug, irritating, contemptible Doug, had this power to inflame her senses until she yielded in his arms. Even less fair was that he knew the effect of his kisses on her and took advantage of her weakness for his own amusement. The humiliating thought brought her head sharply up.

There was a wry awareness in the blue eyes that glinted down at her. "We're still not very good at keeping truces, are we?" Before she could respond to his unexpected question, he asked another. "If my uncle marries your mother, what does that make us?"

"Enemies."

Doug ran a finger across her throbbing lips. "You're supposed to love thine enemy," he said. And then he was gone. Out into the cold night, disappearing into a whirling curtain of blowing snowflakes. A new storm had moved in.

The next couple of days were remarkably Doug-free. A fact that Samantha viewed with mixed feelings. What had taken place the night she'd dined with his parents had done nothing to mend the rift between her and Doug. In spite of his comment to his parents that Samantha considered him as one of the family, it was clear that Doug himself didn't believe it. Her sin of omission had not been forgiven. Regrettably. And yet, at the same time, Samantha felt a sense of relief. Memories of the evening haunted her. Doug's lips warm against hers... Such memories were dangerous to dwell on. Such behaviour would be dangerous to repeat. Doug's kisses, Doug's arms—if she wasn't careful, they could become a fatal addiction.

The inn was enjoying a rare moment of quiet. Mary, Edna and Louise had gone home, the guests were all out on the slopes or exploring the shops, and the phone was not ringing. General and Mrs. Clayborne had departed yesterday, and Mrs. Arden would be coming home soon.

Life would be back to normal at the Hummingbird Inn. No, that wasn't true. Samantha pensively tapped a pencil against her chin. This winter had changed everything. David had Lynda. As for her mother, Ike Clayborne had pressed his suit and been accepted.

And then there was Samantha. Always a bridesmaid... On the outside, looking in. She shook her head to rid herself of such outmoded thoughts. Today's woman wasn't measured by her ability to catch a husband. Samantha doodled on a piece of scrap paper. Her problem wasn't the lack of a husband. It was nothing more than spring fever, being penned in by the snow, a longing for summer meadows and wild blue columbine. She looked outside. The wind flung bursts of snow against the windows. Riding up the ski lifts would be brutal in the freezing wind. It was a day for lovers to curl up in front of the fireplace, exchanging confidences.

She started to wonder what Doug was doing, then, catching herself, forcibly turned her thoughts to this evening and her mother's birthday. They planned to take a cake and presents to the hospital. Samantha smiled. The negligee she'd purchased for her mother was wickedly indecent, but Mrs. Arden still had the figure to wear it.

The look on her mother's face was everything that Samantha had hoped for. "Sammie! I'm too old to wear something like this. It's indecent," her mother protested.

"Why don't you let Ike be the judge of that," Samantha teased.

Mrs. Arden shook her head at Doug. "I thought you were going to make sure that Sammie behaved while I was in here."

"It takes a bigger man than Doug for that," Samantha said.

"I think the word you want is braver," David said with a laugh. "Doug is too fond of his head."

Samantha favored her brother with a grimace as her mother opened the next present. Ike had dragged

Samantha on a round of jewelry shops, so the diamond ring he gave her mother was no surprise to Samantha. The gift from David and Lynda turned out to be a warm robe that exactly matched Samantha's gift. "The saleslady told me what you'd bought," Lynda confessed.

Only Doug's gift was left, and all eyes turned expectantly toward him. He grinned. "I know what you're all thinking. What's left to give this woman who has everything? I admit that Ike's gift would ordinarily be hard to top, but as it happens what's in here..." he tapped the large flat box "... is going to be Lucy's favorite gift." Amid boos and cries of scorn, he handed Mrs. Arden the box. "Happy birthday, Lucy."

The look on her mother's face as she lifted aside the tissue paper told Samantha that Doug had not erred in his judgment. Tears gathered in her mother's eyes. "How did you ever...?" Mrs. Arden held up a large frame. Three photographs of Samantha had been matted and arranged in a triangle. Three totally different portraits of Samantha. Mrs. Arden's mouth quivered. "Doug, they're wonderful. Sammie in all her moods. You've captured her spirit. I can almost hear her speak."

"Maybe it's best we can't." David pointed to one of the pictures. "She looks pretty annoyed about something here."

Doug had refused to show Samantha the proofs, claiming she'd never be objective. She frowned at them now. One appeared to be of a saucy child who was all teeth. In another she was pensive, the snow clinging to her lashes. The one David had referred to... "I suppose that's your idea of a joke," she said to Doug.

"It's an honest picture," he said. "What did you want? Some stiff studio shot with all the life and personality of a dead fish?"

Ike put his arm around her. "All I know is, if I hang these pictures of my new daughter in our house, I'll have every male within a thousand miles camping on my doorstep in hopes Sammie will grace us with her presence." He squeezed her shoulders. "A woman with a little fire in her eyes puts a man on his mettle."

Ike's words lightened the atmosphere, and Samantha smiled gratefully at him. "If Mother changes her mind about this wedding," she said, "I'll marry you myself."

"Now she tells me." Ike heaved a heavy sigh. "Lucy will never give up a great catch like me. Even for her own daughter."

Mrs. Arden threw a ribbon at him.

Ike stayed on at the hospital and David and Lynda had another engagement, so Doug was forced to offer Samantha a ride home. He whistled tunelessly on the long drive as if she weren't even there. Back at the inn, Samantha stepped hastily from the car. Inside the warm foyer, she concentrated on reading the messages that Edna had left for her. None were important. None mattered. Nothing mattered. Slowly she shuffled the message slips. A tear slid down her cheek and she brushed it away. What was wrong with her anyway? Maybe she was coming down with Edna's flu. Perhaps a cup of tea...

Her back to the door that opened into the yard, she put on the kettle. When she turned around, Doug was standing there. Startled, her hand flew to her throat. "I didn't hear you come in."

"Sorry," he said, crossing to the cupboard and taking down two mugs. "I thought you might be expecting me."

"Why would I?"

"Having tea after some event, discussing what happened ... It's a Arden family tradition." His smile was skewed. "Even for a provisional family member like me."

"How many times do I have to apologize for that?" She handed him the tin of tea. "I wasn't implying that you didn't belong or that I was surprised that you were helping. I just didn't want you to think that I was taking you for granted." A sudden thought struck her. "That picture was your revenge, wasn't it?"

"What picture?"

"The one of me looking like a shrew."

Doug laughed. "That picture shows precisely the way you look about ninety per cent of the time you're around me."

Samantha stirred her tea slowly. "Do I really?"

Doug's smile faded. "It wasn't intended to be an insult, Sammie. As Ike said, it's a portrait of a woman with fire."

"Too much fire." Her own smile was fleeting. "I wish I were more like Lynda. So calm, so in control." She stared down into her swirling tea. "The way I act, the things I say... No wonder you think I'm horrid."

"Sammie, Sammie. What is this orgy of introspection? Have you caught Edna's flu?"

"See? Even if I tried to reform, you wouldn't take me seriously. Which only proves what a pain I've been. I'm sorry."

"Oh, no, you don't. Not that damned wobble." Doug came around the table and raised her face, a finger under her chin. "Let me tell you a secret. The first time I came home with David and met you, I was green with envy. I'd always wanted a little sister."

"Before you knew me better, you mean." She couldn't meet his eyes. Not when his voice was filled with gentle amusement.

"Before I learned that little sisters are bratty pests. You couldn't pay me to have one now. They're always in the way. Always demanding attention." The gentleness was gone.

"Isn't it time for you to go home?"

"Little sisters are dumped on you." His hands dropped to her shoulders. "I'd rather have a friend. Will you be my friend, Samantha?"

Friend. It had a nice sound. Samantha tested it on her tongue as she straightened up from her chores and rubbed the small of her back. Her mother was coming home from the hospital tomorrow. Mrs. Arden would be thrilled with how polite Samantha and Doug were to each other. They deferred to the other's opinions, they avoided controversial topics, they refused to challenge or antagonize each other. They didn't kiss.

Samantha sank to the rim of the bathtub. They didn't kiss. Discontent nagged at her and she thrust it aside. Why would they kiss? The only reason Doug had ever kissed her was because he was trying to use his masculine charm to dominate her. Now that they weren't locked in a battle for supremacy, he didn't need to resort to such reprehensible tactics. And it wasn't as if she had enjoyed his kisses. She'd endured them through necessity. The first time he'd kissed her, if she'd fought him off, David would have discovered Doug's painful secret. Doug's secret. The reason he'd kissed her to begin with. He'd thought she was Lynda. How could Samantha possibly go weak at the knees at the memory of a kiss that hadn't even been intended for her?

Her eyes watered. The cleaning solution must be too strong. She went over to the window and opened it. Icy air flowed into the small room, bringing voices from the other side of the yard. Samantha bent down and looked out. Lynda and Doug were standing on the back stoop of his house. As Samantha watched, Doug put his hands on Lynda's shoulders. Lynda rose up on tiptoe. She was going to kiss Doug.

Samantha turned back to the sink. Doug had said that he was hopelessly in love with Lynda. Hopelessly in love. Samantha scrubbed blindly at the white porcelain. Was there ever a more dismal phrase? And Lynda. Samantha had believed her sister-in-law to be crazy about David. Had Doug's unswerving devotion proved irresistible? The dinner with Doug's parents... Samantha should have paid more attention to her suspicions that night. Suspicions that had been forgotten in the face of Doug's accusations about her and Ike.

She sniffed and rubbed her nose with the back of her hand. A hand wearing a blue rubber glove. A present from Doug. She held her hands out in front of her. The gloves somehow defined their relationship. No flowers or chocolates such as he'd undoubtedly bestowed upon Lynda and all the other blond bimbos in his life. Not that Lynda was a blond bimbo. At least, Samantha hadn't thought so. But if she was considering an affair with Doug when she was married to David... Doug. It was all his fault. Tempting Lynda. Why didn't he leave her alone? There must be women in the world who would massage his ego with a pretense of weakness and dependence. Women who would never argue with him or compete with him or eclipse him. Women who looked fragile and pretty in pale pink.

Women totally unlike Samantha. She certainly wasn't interested in a man whose ego was so delicate that he was afraid of a strong woman. A man so insecure that his self-image couldn't survive a lost card game or a smaller fish. A man who... She sniffed again and looked down at her hands. A man who gave her blue rubber gloves. A man who donned a silly apron to serve breakfast to help her out. A man who cleared dishes and made beds with blankets so tight that quarters would bounce off them. A man who created beauty for a house-bound elderly woman. A man who folded napkins into unusual shapes. A man who was strong and independent and adventuresome and exciting. A man who teased her and tormented her. Tormented her with his kisses.

She brushed away a tear with the back of her wrist as the unwelcome truth refused to go away. She'd fallen in love with Douglas Patton Clayborne Jr. The man who loved her brother's wife. A man who considered Samantha Arden an unwelcome pest and a spoiled brat. He'd told her more than once that she angered, annoyed, infuriated and drove him crazy. She was crazy herself to even be thinking such nonsense. Doug would laugh himself silly. The ultimate joke. And it was on her.

"You trying to wear the porcelain off that sink?" Louise stood in the doorway, her brown eyes sharp behind wire-framed glasses. "What's wrong? Looks as if you've been crying."

"I just splashed some soap in my eyes," Samantha lied.

"Uh-huh. Lucy's too involved with her boyfriend to see what's been going on around here, but I'm not blind. Me and Edna and Mary been talking it over, but you don't want our advice, so I'm not going to give you any. I only have one question. Since when is Samantha Arden a quitter?"

"I'm not," Samantha protested, but she was speaking to an empty doorway. "I'm not," she said again.

CHAPTER NINE

NERVOUSLY Samantha wiped her hands on her apron. Doug had gone to Denver for the afternoon, but he'd told Ike he'd be home around six. She checked the clock again. It was almost six. The spicy smells of spaghetti sauce and garlic bread wafted from Doug's kitchen. The table was set with her mother's best lace cloth and her grandmother's floral china. She'd stolen the best flowers from those meant to decorate the breakfast tables at the inn. The wine had been recommended by the man at the shop, and Doug's glassware stood ready to be filled. All that was needed was Doug.

Samantha poked the fire, sending sparks flying up the chimney. Not that the fire needed attending. It was simply that she was too nervous to remain still. If only Doug didn't laugh at her. If only he gave her a chance. She'd prove to him that he didn't need Lynda. That Samantha could be exactly the woman he needed. She would be calm and gentle. She'd let him open the wine, carry the heavy pot from the stove, pull out her chair, make their decisions. Standing in front of the mirror by Doug's door, she fussed with her hair, pinning a stray curl up here and there. No smart-aleck remarks, she reminded the image looking back at her, no sarcastic put-downs, no disagreeing with his opinions. She'd gaze worshipfully into his eyes, smooth his weary brow, kiss his feet—her image gazed reproachfully back at her. Letting your attitude slip, aren't you? it seemed to ask.

166

She had to curb her sarcastic tongue. Taking off her apron, she tossed it on a nearby chair. At least outwardly, she was the essence of femininity in a violet-colored velvet gown, purchased only this afternoon in an exclusive downtown boutique. Samantha had not forgotten Doug's reaction to the coral dress, and the violet gown had long sleeves and a neckline that dipped indecently low with a shadowy V that called attention to rounded flesh. The long skirt clung sensuously to her bare legs as she headed back to the kitchen. Footsteps echoed up the staircase. Doug was home. The speedy tempo of her heart sent waves of her delicate floral perfume into the air. Quickly she pressed the button on his stereo. Dreamy love songs poured forth as Doug inserted his key in the lock.

Samantha lost her courage and bolted for the kitchen, picking up the apron en route. By the time Doug came in, she was stirring the spaghetti, apron in place, her back to the door.

"What's going on?" Doug came over to the stove, sniffing with appreciation.

"Ike's eating with Mother, and he talked me into feeding you." Her heart beat so fast that it amazed her that she was able to speak in a normal voice.

"Let me guess. You're practicing your cooking on me?"

Samantha looked at the center of his chest. "Do you mind?"

"Not if it tastes like it smells." He went toward his bedroom, then hesitated before opening the door. "You haven't been in here, have you?"

Samantha shook her head. "I've been too busy cooking to snoop." She winced as he snorted and went into his room. Already she'd violated the first rule of how to sweet-talk your way into a man's heart. Going on the attack was not part of her plan. She looked down at the apron which more than adequately covered her plunging neckline. At least, she amended, not that kind of attack. In a burst of resolution, she discarded the apron again.

Doug came out of his room, carefully shutting the door behind him. Samantha glided past him with their salads, the vegetables artistically arranged on the plates. "Looks great," he said.

"A little something I learned in Europe."

"An educational two years."

She handed him the wine and corkscrew. "Okay? Todd, down at the liquor store, said you liked it." She set the glasses in front of him.

"That's not my tape," Doug said, over the violin strains.

"No. Just a little something I picked up today."

He poured the wine and handed her a glass. "You've been a busy little bee today, haven't you?" Lifting his glass in a silent toast, he took a drink. "The dress a little something you picked up today, too?"

Samantha carried the spaghetti sauce to the table and twirled around, close enough to Doug that the velvet skirt brushed his legs. "Yes. Like it?"

"I'm not sure." There was a thoughtful look on his face.

"Men." Samantha patted his cheek as she swept back to the kitchen. "Could you please help me a minute? The noodles need to be drained, and the pot's too heavy for me."

"How did you get it to the stove?"

"Empty. I added the water a glassful at a time," she lied. Doug gave her a funny look, but did her bidding.

Standing at his side with a bowl for the noodles, Samantha brushed against his arm. The sleeve of his shirt was smooth and cool against her bare skin above the neckline. "Thank you." She peered up at him from beneath lowered lids. "What would women do without men?"

Doug frowned and dumped the noodles into the bowl. At the table he seemed to take in the elegant setting and the burning candles for the first time. "Special occasion?"

"No. I just think this makes the food taste better." She lifted up her napkin. "Well? Regimental stripes or whatever you called it. Not as nicely done as when you folded them, but not bad, do you think?"

"I'm not sure what I think." He sipped his wine.

Samantha passed him the hot garlic bread. "How was Denver?"

"The same as usual. Half successful and half frustrating. The lab lost some of my film. You remember when I filmed those deer over by Frisco where they were bedding down?" When she nodded, he added, "That's the film they can't find."

"Oh, no. All of it?"

"Fortunately not. Of course," he grinned wryly, "I always assume what's lost was my best stuff."

Samantha was genuinely dismayed and asked him if that sort of thing happened often. Soon she was engrossed in the stories Doug told of his adventures and mishaps. He'd tripped over rocks, logs, a sleeping javelina and a coiled rattlesnake. He'd fallen into cacti, been stung by numerous insects and been chased by everything from an angry bison to a mother hawk to farmers' dogs. She shook her head. "You certainly lead an intrepid life. I had no idea it was so fraught with hazard.''

Doug pushed his empty plate away and leaned back in his chair. ''Nothing in the past has been as interesting as this evening. Or, I'm beginning to suspect, as hazardous.''

Samantha stood up and reached for his plate. ''I don't know what you mean. I thought you might be tired and would appreciate having dinner ready when you arrived home.'' She paused. ''There's coffee and apple pie.''

''Just coffee,'' he said.

When she returned with two mugs, the living-room lights were turned low, and Doug was fiddling with the stereo. ''Putting on some longer-playing music,'' he said, sitting down on the sofa. Taking his mug from her, he pulled her down beside him. ''I hate to be interrupted in the middle of something to go change the music,'' he said smoothly.

''Oh.'' Her voice was practically a squeak. She took a big gulp of coffee.

Doug took her mug and set it beside his on the low table in front of them. ''Dinner was delicious, but it's the after-dinner entertainment that I've been looking forward to.''

A feeling of panic stole over Samantha at the blatant sensuality in Doug's voice. ''I—I have to do the dishes,'' she protested nervously. Somehow she'd lost control of the evening.

''They'll keep.'' Doug turned her on the sofa so that she was facing him, half lying across his lap. ''I like that perfume,'' he said, his hands busy in her hair.

''I—I know.'' His touch was light, but her scalp tingled. Hairpins dropped to the table with little pings. Her heart seemed to ping in time with them, and then her hair was loose around her face, and Doug wove his fingers through it, urging her closer to him. Her eyelids drifted shut and he dropped light kisses on them. And then she was lying on her back pinned between the back of the sofa and Doug's long, hard body.

He was staring down at her, his head propped up on one hand. "Would I be anywhere close if I guessed you wore this dress because you knew this," a warm finger slowly outlined the V of her neckline, "would drive me crazy?"

"You might be." The look in his eyes held her captive.

He toyed with the tab of the zipper. "Isn't having the zipper so accessible right here in front living a little dangerously?"

Samantha shifted a little to one side. The movement brought the side of one of her breasts against Doug's hand. "For you or for me?"

Doug laughed softly before lowering his head. "Meaning I'll get my head knocked off if I give in to temptation." His lips brushed against the sensitive skin beneath her ear as he spoke.

Responding to his gentle nudge, Samantha tipped back her head, exposing her neck to his lips. "I didn't say that," she managed to gasp.

"You forget. I know you." He pressed his mouth against the frantic beating of her pulse at the base of her neck. "Frightened?" His hand was warm above her waistline.

Samantha shivered with pleasure. "No." Doug slid down her zip, pressing the metal against her bare skin as he did so. Her nerves screamed with pleasure and anticipation.

"Maybe you should be." Doug's voice was smooth as silk.

"Why?" She wanted his lips on hers.

His hand slid between the dress and her skin, his fingers closing about the fullness of a swollen breast, his thumb and forefinger rolling the nipple between them. Finally his lips sought hers, and she welcomed his questing tongue. In the background a thirties torch singer sang of love and pain in a sultry voice that hinted of satin sheets and silk lingerie. Doug's lips slid from hers, trailing down bare skin and leaving burning flesh in their wake. Her body arched in invitation. An invitation Doug accepted, his searing mouth closing over a hard, sensitive tip. Just when she was sure she would explode with pleasure, Doug lifted his head. "Do you want to do it here or in the bedroom?" he asked.

Samantha opened her eyes, blinking rapidly to dispel the mists of passion which blurred her vision. "What did you say?"

"I said, you can strip down and we can do it here, or we can go into the bedroom like civilized people. It makes no difference to me."

She stared up at him in disbelief. His words were cold and crude, but they couldn't begin to match the contempt in his eyes as his gaze slowly traveled the length of her body, stripping away her remaining clothing. "What's the matter with you?" One of his hands still fondled a breast. Samantha struck the hand aside and clutched the edges of her gown together in front. "Why are you looking at me like that?"

Doug brushed aside her trembling hands and tugged her zip abruptly into place. "I warned you not to play your games with me." In one lithe move, he was off the sofa and looking down at her. His anger was all the more terrible for being held so tightly under control.

Shivering, as much from confusion as from the loss of Doug's heated body, Samantha sat up, her feet resting on the floor. She shook her head slowly, numbly, from side to side. "I'm not playing any games. I'm not."

Her words had little effect on him. His face was implacable, his eyes burning with wrath. She flinched at the loathing in his voice. "Don't lie to me. Samantha Arden and all this." He waved his arm toward the kitchen. "Candlelight, soft music, good food, a sexy dress—you might have succeeded if you hadn't got so carried away that you acted totally out of character. Did you think that the sight of you hanging out of that dress was enough to blind me to your real intentions? Or did you count on the wine and your perfume to befuddle my wits?" He snorted before mimicking, "The pot is too heavy for me. Todd said you liked this wine." His voice returned to normal. "Even pretending that I can fold napkins better than you can. You have never since I've known you admitted that I can do anything better than you." He was pacing back and forth in front of the sofa, his anger not allowing him to remain still. "You'd die first."

"I didn't——"

"Didn't what?" He towered over her. "Didn't think I was smart enough to catch on?"

She shrank back into the sofa. "On to what?"

He looked at her with scorching contempt. "I knew when I forced you to go along with this fake engagement I'd have to pay." Pulling her to her feet, his fingers pressed painfully into her shoulders. "I thought it would be worth any price just to see you do my bidding. But I never dreamed you'd go to this extreme. Abandoning your self-respect to get even. Just how far were you willing to go in your pretense of seducing me? Did you think it would be amusing to toy with me until I totally lost control? Is that when you planned to slap my face? Or perhaps you had something even more diabolical in mind? Like shouting rape?'' He gave her a sharp shake. ''Am I right?''

The pain was too intense for tears. Not from his grip or his shaking—from his accusations. That Doug could believe she was capable of such treachery turned all hope to ashes. He gave her another shake, reminding her that he was waiting for her answer. ''No,'' she cried, ''you're wrong!''

''Don't lie to me,'' he said in a heavy voice. ''I thought we could be friends, but it's too late, isn't it? After twelve years of animosity, it's impossible for you and me to ever feel anything for each other besides dislike, anger, irritation and possibly, just possibly, on good days, a kind of wary respect for the other's capacity to hurt and frustrate.'' He dropped his hands with a muttered curse and turned away.

Samantha stumbled blindly over to the dining table. Pain and humiliation washed over her. She'd made a fool of herself. Doug could never love her. He disliked her. A sound, half laugh, half sob, caught in her throat. Dislike. A pallid emotion. If he'd said hate, she might have felt hope. But dislike. An emotion for dead flies and weeds in the vegetable garden.

''What do you think you're doing?''

She bit her lip. ''The dishes.''

''The hell with them. Get out of here. Go home before I forget I'm supposed to be a gentleman.'' Numbly she turned toward the door. ''Not like that,'' he said through clenched teeth. ''You look as if you've been doing exactly what you thought you could trick me into believing you were going to do.'' He pushed her toward his bedroom.

"Go fix your face or whatever it is women do." When she fumbled with the doorknob, he made an exasperated sound. Then, just as she managed to turn the knob, he cursed beneath his breath and shoved her aside. "Just a minute."

She leaned against the wall, hardly caring, his words still ringing in her head. Impossible for him to ever feel anything for her but dislike. A thump came from Doug's bedroom and then he called for her to come in. He was standing in front of a picture he'd obviously just removed from the wall. It didn't take the angry look of challenge on his face to tell her what the photograph was of. Or rather, who. Lynda. He must have photographed her before she met David.

Samantha stared down at the combs on Doug's bathroom sink until she found the energy to drag one through her hair. A splash of cold water brought a little color to her face. Not enough, but it would have to do.

Back in the dining room Doug was pouring himself another glass of wine. Wordlessly she took her coat from his cupboard by the door and slipped into it. Her hand was on the door when he spoke. "Why? That's all I want to know. Why? Okay, so we've never been friends, but I thought at least we'd reached a kind of cease-fire. So why now?"

She forced herself to turn and face him. She could never tell him the truth, but perhaps he was entitled to a partial truth. "I saw you and Lynda on your back step this morning."

His body went rigid. "So?"

"She kissed you and I th-thought . . ." Her voice died away at the fury on his face.

"You thought the worst," he ground out. "You always do." He shot her a sudden look. "Are you trying to tell me that you came over here to distract me? All this heavy seduction stuff was nothing more than another glass of cold water in my lap?''

She shook her head. ''No. I thought—that is... I know I'm nothing like Lynda... but I thought... if you were otherwise occupied... She and David just need time to strengthen their marriage...'' At the look of black fury on his face, she almost fled, but she forced herself to finish the halting explanation. ''I thought—if I went to bed with you—if we were actually having an affair...you wouldn't need her so much.''

''Lord!'' Doug exploded. ''Not only were you planning to sacrifice your body to save your brother's marriage, but you intended it to be an act of charity toward me.'' He knocked a chair across the room. ''You'd better get out before I break your stupid little neck in half.''

He didn't need to tell her twice. As she crossed the yard between the houses, the night air was frigid and her body shook, as with a fever. The lobby and hallway were empty, the sounds of the television emanating from the parlor. Samantha gave Louise a quick flip of her hand from the parlor doorway, but she couldn't stop to speak to her. Not now. Louise would know that she could go home and she'd leave any messages on the desk. Tomorrow would be soon enough to deal with them. Please, let there be no one in the hall who wanted to talk. Her silent prayer was answered.

In her room she shrugged off her coat and let it fall to the floor. Her dress was next. Kicked aside to a corner, it could rot there. Her flannel nightshirt covered her to below her knees, but it failed to warm her shivering body. She curled up beneath the covers. If only sleep would come quickly, allowing her to escape from the shambles of the evening.

Foolish hope. Thoughts, memories, emotions, all tumbled painfully over her, refusing to be held at bay any longer. What an idiot she had been. Hadn't twelve years of Doug saying that he didn't like her, that he didn't want her around, taught her anything? She only had to look at the women who had attracted Doug through the years to know that he'd never want someone like her. He'd always gone for tall, cool blondes. He'd never been attracted to short, ill-tempered shrews who were unable to fake dependency and who would never lose a tennis match or chess game simply to prove they were the weaker sex.

Not even for one evening had she been able to fool Doug into believing that she could be other than she was. It had been crazy of her to even consider it. For that matter, it was crazy of her to even want to. If she wasn't Doug's type, so was the reverse true. She didn't want a man who feared women who were equals. She didn't want a man who had to be buoyed up by the worship of a woman. She didn't want... Tears streamed down her face.

Who was she trying to kid? She did want Doug. He wasn't all those things. He was strong, secure, self-confident. He didn't need a woman like Lynda. The stupid jerk. He was just too darned stupid and stubborn to know what he needed. Lynda was right for David, but she was totally wrong for Doug. Doug loved Lynda for her perfection. No wonder Lynda had rejected him for David's more accepting love. David would love Lynda when her hair was a mess, when she had the flu, when her stockings had a run... He would love her perfection, her flaws, her pimples, her blemishes.

Just as Samantha loved Doug. She smiled through her tears. Heaven knew she wasn't blind to Doug's faults. He was arrogant, opinionated, argumentative, always had to win, be right...and she loved every arrogant, opinionated bone in his body. He was the perfect man for her and she was the perfect woman for him. Maybe they didn't always act in perfect harmony. That would bore Doug as much as it would bore her. Lynda would bore Doug. The thought came from nowhere but she knew it was true. Her mother was right—Doug was reserved. Lynda could never smash through that wall. Samantha could.

Except that Doug wouldn't let her. Her pillow was damp, and she turned it over. If only she'd come to her senses earlier; realized what Doug meant to her. She should have tried to be more accommodating. But Doug didn't want her more accommodating. He didn't want her at all. She had to face the painful truth. Doug had known Samantha for twelve years—long enough to know how much he disliked her. She wiped her eyes. Maybe she would go back to Switzerland.

A soft knock sounded at her door. Samantha ignored it, unable to deal with any of the inn's guests now. The knocking grew louder. She buried her head under her pillow, willing the unseen intruder to go away.

"Samantha, open this door." The whispered order came from Doug.

He must have thought of something else to yell at her for. She pulled the covers over her head. He could just go away. She had no intention of talking to him. Ever again. The weight on her bed took her by surprise. She hadn't heard her door open. Lifting the pillow and covers from her head, she glared at Doug. "Get out of my bedroom."

"I want to talk to you," he said in a low voice.

"I don't want to talk to you." She flopped the pillow over her head again.

Doug jerked it from her and threw it across the room. "I said," he ground out, "I want to talk to you."

Childishly she put her hands over her ears and squeezed closed her eyelids.

He grabbed her hands and held them to his chest. "Don't push me too far," he said, his face inches from hers. "I'm not in the mood for any of your fun and games."

"You already made that perfectly clear this evening, so you can go home." Forgetting the time, she'd raised her voice. Overhead bedsprings creaked. Belatedly lowering her voice, she spat, "Will you get out of here before you wake everyone up?"

"Not until we talk." He'd been speaking in a low tone, but now he chose to speak normally.

Samantha glared at him. "I know what you're doing. Go ahead. Wake up the whole house. Have everyone down here standing in the doorway. Invite them all in. I don't care. But I am not going to talk to you, and I'm not going to listen to you. I don't even want to talk to you again. You are the most irritating, stubborn, arrogant..." Her heart lurched as Doug stood up. She whipped up her anger. It was her only defense against tears. Only the dark room prevented Doug from seeing the betraying marks already on her cheeks.

Doug whipped the covers off the bed.

"What are you doing?"

"I said I wanted to talk to you. And, one way or another, I intend to." He jerked her from the bed and wrapped a blanket about her body, binding her arms against her side.

"You—you b-beast!" Samantha was almost incoherent with rage. "Let go of me!" Doug hoisted her over his shoulder and headed for her bedroom door. "Put me down!" she shrieked, trying to free her legs from his iron grip.

In the hall, doors popped open and guests stood there, eyes boggling with astonishment at the spectacle before them. Doug greeted everyone as casually as if he were taking an afternoon stroll. Samantha struggled furiously. Managing to free one arm, she repeatedly punched Doug in the middle of his back.

He halted abruptly. "Good evening, Ike. Sorry if we awakened you."

"Quite all right, my boy. I wouldn't have missed this for the world. All you all right, Sammie?"

"No, I'm not all right. Make him put me down." Twisting around, she sank her teeth into Doug's shoulder.

Doug whirled, almost banging her head into the wall. "I'm sorry we disturbed you, but if you don't mind we'd like a little privacy." No one would argue with Doug when he used that cold, formal tone of voice, and Samantha wasn't surprised to hear doors quietly shutting all along the corridor. "Now, you brat." He swatted her on her bottom. "Don't bite."

She was swathed in too many layers of blanket for his action to hurt, but that failed to lessen the indignity. "I'm going to kill you," she promised.

"Perhaps you ought to put her down," Ike said.

"You heard her." Doug gave a short laugh. "I do and she'll kill me."

"You can hardly spend the rest of your life carrying her around on your shoulder, so I suggest you come up with some solution."

"I have every intention of doing exactly that," Doug assured his uncle. "I'm either going to strangle her or marry her. I haven't decided which yet. Quit wriggling," he snarled to Samantha, "or I'll drop you on your head."

"Ah," Ike said. "True love. Lucy will be pleased. She's been anticipating an announcement for some time." His voice changed. "Doug, is Sammie all right? She's gone awfully still." He stepped around and stared horrified into Samantha's face. "This has suddenly ceased to be amusing, Douglas. This poor girl is crying her eyes out."

"Don't be misled," said Doug dryly. "This poor girl, as you call her, is capable of taking on a grizzly bear and winning. Never mind, we're leaving."

Back in his apartment, Doug dumped Samantha on his bed. Up two flights of stairs and he was barely breathing heavily. He tossed a box of paper tissues on the bed beside her. She loudly blew her nose, refusing to look at him.

"After I thought it over, I decided that your explanation earlier this evening left something to be desired," Doug said.

"I don't care what you thought."

"Then why are you crying?"

"You hit me."

Doug snorted. "That little tap didn't hurt you and you know it."

"I don't know anything any more." She blew her nose again, her face resolutely turned away from him.

"That's the first time I've ever heard you admit that." Doug left the room. When he returned he sat down on the edge of the bed. "And I'll bet I never hear it again." He reached for her chin and, holding her face immobile, bathed the tears from her face with a warm flannel.

His weight was tipping the mattress, and she struggled to keep from sliding toward him. "You won't. I'm going back to Switzerland." She stared belligerently at him.

"You think so?" His smile was rueful. "I used to think the worst thing you could do to me was apologize. That damned wobble, but..." he shook his head "...tears are worse. No, don't..." He dabbed at the fresh stream that poured from her eyes and then turned and leaned back against the headboard. "Come here."

"I want to go home."

"Not until we talk." Doug tugged the blanket from beneath her and smoothed it over her legs. "Okay?"

"No. I have nothing to say to you and..." her voice caught on a sob "...you've said quite enough to me."

Doug crossed his long legs on the bed. "We're going to talk whether you want to or not. If we'd been honest with each other earlier this evening, and if you hadn't jumped to some wild conclusions about——"

"Me!" She stared at him in total disbelief. "What about you? Thinking that I..." Her gaze shifted to somewhere behind him as she fought the tears swelling her throat.

"All right. Me, too. At least," he added cautiously, "I think I probably jumped to a few erroneous conclusions tonight."

"A few!" Samantha sniffed. "You didn't see me kissing anyone on my back step."

"Okay. I guess it's only fair we discuss Lynda first. After all, it was my so-called passion for her that started this whole mess."

"So-called!" Samantha's voice rose indignantly. "You were crazy in love with her."

Doug shrugged. "I certainly thought so. She's probably the most beautiful woman I know. She's cool and elegant and everything I thought I wanted in a woman, but I was wrong. My eyes approved of her, but my heart went untouched. Do you remember David saying that when he fell in love with her he wanted to shout it from the highest mountain?" At her slight nod, he continued, "At the time, I thought David was being a little dramatic."

"And now?" She concentrated on the tissue she was pleating between her fingers.

"And now I know what love really is. It's when an argumentative, curly-haired brat drives a man so crazy he doesn't know the difference between up and down." Suddenly she was on her back and he was towering over her. "It's when a man tastes certain lips..." he pressed a light kiss against the corner of her mouth "...and develops an intense craving for them..." his lips moved over to the other side "...and starts going berserk at the thought of those lips being kissed by another man. I wanted to wring his neck every time you smiled at Barlowe," he growled beneath her ear, "and I was ready to sock my own uncle." He nipped her earlobe with his teeth. "The only thing that saved him was getting engaged to Lucy."

"You can't love me," she said desperately. "You think I'm a spoiled brat."

He nudged aside the neckline of her nightshirt and burned a trail of kisses across her collarbone. "You are."

Samantha shoved him aside and sat up, glaring down at him. "You yelled at me and hit me. You kidnapped me. That's not love. That's—that's..." She couldn't think what it was.

Doug pulled her back down beside him. "I didn't hit you. As for the rest, it was the act of a desperate man." His mouth cut off any more objections.

Not that Samantha could come up with any. Doug's kisses had sapped her resistance and swept aside her ability to think. All she knew was a desperate need to feel his arms holding her tight while his lips pressed against hers. Doug seemed to read her mind, and Samantha abandoned herself to the taste of Doug's mouth, the feel of his hard body and stroking hands. His mouth left hers and her eyes fluttered open as he raised his head. The flames in his eyes flustered her. His hands were busy with the buttons down the front of her nightshirt and then one hand was warming a breast which swelled to fill his palm. She knew her eyes had betrayed her when Doug chuckled with quiet satisfaction.

She hurriedly looked away. The picture still leaning face against the wall caught her eye, and she froze. Lynda. He'd tried to substitute Samantha for Lynda before. Was that what this was all about? Had what she'd said earlier convinced him that Samantha was perfectly capable of taking care of his needs? She hadn't really meant it. She didn't want him on those terms. Not if Doug still loved Lynda. He'd said he didn't, but . . . "Lynda's visit this morning . . ." she managed to say, pushing his hand away.

He caught her hand in his and raised it to his lips. "Purely professional," he said, nibbling on the edge of her palm. "She wondered if I had any pictures taken on Boreas Pass that she can buy for David's birthday. That's where he proposed to her."

Samantha tried to ignore the erotic sensations that were rocketing up her arm. "Maybe he'd prefer that one."

Doug followed the direction of her gaze. "I doubt it." He rolled off the bed and picked up the picture and set it against the foot of the bed, facing Samantha.

The photograph was of Samantha. One of those taken in the snow, but totally different from the ones Doug had presented to her mother. It was the portrait of a woman who had been well kissed and who was remembering the kiss. At the same time it was clear that she was longing to be kissed again. The photograph simmered with sensuality and desire and promise.

There was a hook on the wall, and Doug hung the picture from it. His back to her as he straightened it, he said, "Your mother really liked those other portraits. Wonder if she'd like a copy of this one?"

Samantha sprang bolt upright on the bed. "You wouldn't!"

"You know better than that."

"That's blackmail."

Doug nodded. "I've also considered telling her that you seduced me the night before David's wedding. And that you've been spending quite a few nights here since she's been in the hospital. She'll insist we get married."

"Why would you do that?" Samantha could barely force the words out.

"Because I love you, you nincompoop."

"No, you don't." Angrily she brushed away a betraying tear. "You think I'm a brat."

"I also happen to think you're cute and funny and hot-tempered and loyal." He sat back down on the bed. "You'll notice I didn't say I thought you were perfect. Just perfectly lovable. I love you when you're wrong, I love you when you're in a bad temper, I love you when you're arrogant——"

"Arrogant!" Samantha gasped. "Look who's talking."

Doug laughed. "All right. So neither one of us is perfect. That may be the only thing we'll agree on in our entire married life. I expect we'll still be arguing on our fiftieth wedding anniversary. I promise you one thing, Sammie: I'll always love you and our life together won't be dull."

Her heart speeded up at the entrancing picture Doug had painted, but it wasn't true. He couldn't love her. Not as desperately as she loved him. His mouth covered hers, his body hard and warm against hers, while his hands wreaked havoc on her ability to reason. His mouth stole away her every breath.

"If you have any thoughts about a long engagement, forget them," Doug said hoarsely.

Her hand rested on his chest. His heart pounded against her palm. "All right." She drew up her fingers and began to draw circles on his skin. "Six months."

He captured her teasing hand and lifted it to his mouth so he could press warm kisses into the palm. "If I had my way, I'd give you six minutes. But Lucy needs a few more days of recuperation and my folks will want to come. One week."

"A week," Samantha meekly agreed. Then the meaning of Doug's words penetrated her daze and she sat upright in bed. At the look in Doug's eyes, she hastily tugged her nightshirt up over one bare shoulder. "No one will believe this."

"Sammie," Doug said in an amused voice, "I think we're the last to know. My mother said that she was so disappointed when she first met you——"

"I knew it." Flopping back down on the bed, she closed her eyes. "She hates me."

He hushed her with his hand. "You sat there so meek and quiet, not at all what she was expecting. Until you called my dad a bully."

She moaned, her eyes squeezed shut in mortification. "They both hate me." With Doug's hand still over her mouth, the words came out garbled.

Doug lifted his hand and kissed her before she could say any more. "They hate you so much that my dad said if I didn't marry you he was disowning me, and my mother made me promise that I'd bring you to visit soon. As for your mother, once when you were eighteen I was furious about something you had done and she laughed and predicted then that I'd end up marrying you."

Samantha turned to kiss the hand that was stroking her cheek. "And what did you say to that?"

"I was horrified at the very idea." His voice deepened. "Lately, however, it's an idea that's been very much on my mind. I love you, Sammie. Will you marry me?"

She wove her fingers through his long brown ones. "It would mean no more tin bathtubs. No more local beauties scrubbing your back."

"I could still have the tin bathtub, only you would be scrubbing my back."

"If you think——" she began indignantly.

"Sammie, shut up," Doug said softly.

"You can't make me..." She knew he could.

HARLEQUIN ROMANCE®

**Harlequin Romance
knows love can be dangerous!**

Don't miss
TO LOVE AND PROTECT (#3223)
by Kate Denton,
the October title in

THE BRIDAL COLLECTION

THE GROOM'S life was in peril.
THE BRIDE was hired to help him.
BUT THEIR WEDDING was *more* than
a business arrangement!

Available this month in
The Bridal Collection
JACK OF HEARTS (#3218)
by Heather Allison
Wherever Harlequin books are sold.

WED-6

BARBARY WHARF

**An exciting six-book series, one title per month
beginning in October, by bestselling author**

*Charlotte
Lamb*

Set in the glamorous and fast-paced world of international
journalism, BARBARY WHARF will take you from the
Sentinel's hectic newsroom to the most thrilling cities in the
world. You'll meet media tycoon Nick Caspian and his
adversary Gina Tyrrell, whose dramatic story of passion and
heartache develops throughout the six-book series.

In book one, BESIEGED (#1498), you'll also meet Hazel and
Piet. Hazel's always had a good word to say about everyone.
Well, almost. She just can't stand Piet Van Leyden, Nick's
chief architect and one of the most arrogant know-it-alls she's
ever met! As far as Hazel's concerned, Piet's a twentieth-
century warrior, and she's the one being besieged!

Don't miss the sparks in the first BARBARY WHARF
book, BESIEGED (#1498), available in October from
Harlequin Presents.

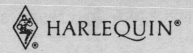 HARLEQUIN®

THE TAGGARTS OF TEXAS!

Harlequin's Ruth Jean Dale brings you
THE TAGGARTS OF TEXAS!

Those Taggart men—strong, sexy and hard to resist...

You've met Jesse James Taggart in FIREWORKS!
Harlequin Romance #3205 (July 1992)

Now meet Trey Smith—he's THE RED-BLOODED YANKEE!
Harlequin Temptation #413 (October 1992)

Then there's Daniel Boone Taggart in SHOWDOWN!
Harlequin Romance #3242 (January 1993)

And finally the Taggarts who started it all—in LEGEND!
Harlequin Historical #168 (April 1993)

Read all the Taggart romances!
Meet all the Taggart men!

Available wherever Harlequin books are sold.

WELCOME TO

The quintessential small town, where everyone
knows everybody else!

Finally, books that capture the pleasure
of tuning in to your favorite TV show!

Join your friends at Tyler in the eighth book, BACHELOR'S PUZZLE by Ginger
Chambers, available in October.

*What do Tyler's librarian and a cosmopolitan architect have in common? What
does the coroner's office have to reveal?*

GREAT READING...GREAT SAVINGS...
AND A FABULOUS FREE GIFT!

Each book set in Tyler is a self-contained love story; together, the twelve novels
stitch the fabric of the community. You can't miss the Tyler books on the shelves
because the covers honor the old American tradition of quilting; each cover
depicts a patch of the large Tyler quilt!

And you can receive a FABULOUS GIFT, ABSOLUTELY FREE, by collecting
proofs-of-purchase found in each Tyler book, *and* use our Tyler coupons to save
on your next TYLER book purchase.

Back by Popular Demand

Janet Dailey
Americana

Janet Dailey takes you on a romantic tour of
America through fifty favorite Harlequin
Presents novels, each one set in a different
state and researched by Janet and her
husband, Bill.

A journey of a lifetime. The perfect
collectible series!

October titles
#41 SOUTH DAKOTA
   Dakota Dreaming
#42 TENNESSEE
   Sentimental Journey